Pike's Path

Pike's Path

A NOVEL

Bland Weaver

atmosphere press

© 2024 Bland Weaver

Published by Atmosphere Press

Cover design by Matthew Fielder

No part of this book may be reproduced without permission from the author except in brief quotations and in reviews. This is a work of fiction, and any resemblance to real places, persons, or events is entirely coincidental.

Atmospherepress.com

About the Author

I grew up in a blue-collar family on Richmond's South Side. My role models were my parents. Mom loved being a stay-at-home mom, and dad worked long hours for forty-six years, managing an automotive repair shop in downtown Richmond. I am the youngest of four children, and my sisters Ruth Ann, Martha and Lynn still reside in Virginia. Even though I live in Richmond's West End, my heart still has strong ties to my old neighborhood. So many early life experiences and relationships are etched in my memory, and they serve to help me with ideas for my writing.

Jahnke Road Baptist Church was an integral force in my formative years. My parents were charter members there, and their legacy of service is still felt at that church today. The Weaver family's social life was centered in church, and there were numerous men and women who served as positive role models for me.

Most kids savor their summer vacations and do not look forward to the start of the school year. I was never one of those kids. My brain was programmed to love new learning opportunities, and that is still true today. I can still recall the names of my Crestwood Elementary teachers—Mrs. Ferguson, Mrs. Caskey, Mrs. Woodcock, Mrs. West, Mrs. Duke and Mrs. Walmsley. I have not crossed paths with any of these dedicated women since I graduated to junior high, but they deserve credit for teaching me the fundamentals that I use for my writing.

Life changed dramatically for me in the seventh grade. That is when my parents enrolled me in a small private school in Chesterfield County. Gill School. The first year was horrible. My classrooms were old and musty, and all of my friends were attending other schools. The second year was a dramatic improvement as I moved into a brand-new building, and better facilities were added. Mrs. Jenny Rodgers was my first English teacher at Gill. She was a no-nonsense disciplinarian whose sole mission to her students was to make sure we learned the English language. That meant grammar and diagramming sentences. Anything I know about word usage or constructing a paragraph is credited to Mrs. Rogers.

During my high school days at Gill, I gained an appreciation for many of the literary classics. Jean Bennett was in the same ranks of the no-nonsense educators, and she was instrumental in encouraging me to develop my writing skills. She helped instill in me the confidence that is so critical in writing a story. Thanks Mrs. Bennett.

Susan Herring was another of my high school English teachers who helped me with the creative side of writing. She had great patience and was kindness personified. Thanks Mrs. Herring.

The years at Gill were some of the best of my life. In 1983 the school closed, but the spirit of my classmates, teachers and coaches holds a special place in my heart.

The University of Richmond was the only college that I wanted to attend. I made a good choice, and I am forever grateful to my parents for sacrificing to pay for my education. During these years most of my writing was devoted to research papers and essay answers on history exams. The history department at Richmond was blessed with extraordinary talent. Dr. Barry Westin, Dr. Martin Ryle, Dr. John Gordon, Dr. John Rilling, Dr. Emory Bogle. These men took the time to encourage me to pursue my writing whether it be in academia or just for fun. Many thanks to all of these distinguished gentlemen.

The pristine beauty of the Richmond campus was one of the main reasons that I selected that school. Joining a fraternity was a life altering decision for me. I am part of the Sigma

Chi brotherhood, and many of us stay close to one another to this day.

After college I entered the teaching profession and taught U.S. and world history for eight years. Those years will always be special to me, and the teachers and students that I had the privilege to work with are some of the best people I have ever known.

For the past thirty-five years, I have been an independent investment advisor. I have been blessed beyond my imagination with the best clients that any advisor could hope for.

About twenty years ago, one of my dearest friends, Mark Hyland, joined me for a golf trip to Myrtle Beach. During conversation, I mentioned that I had an idea for a novel. He encouraged me to put it down on paper. Because I have always respected him, I took his advice to heart and wrote my first novel. Since then, I have written two more.

A fellow writer and long-time friend, Doug Dunnevant, recently published a novel, so I approached him for some advice. He referred me to the capable hands at Atmosphere Press. All of the folks at Atmosphere have been kind, patient and informative. They will have to put up with me again when I decide to publish my other two works.

A big thank you goes out to my niece, Rebekah. Word processing is not my specialty, so my process is to write everything down on legal pads. Then I give the pads to Rebekah, and she toils through my less than beautiful handwriting and types the pages into a Word document. It's hard to teach an old dog new tricks. Thanks Rebekah.

My sons, Eli and Zach, are lights in my life. They may not know it, but they are great inspirations to me, and they occupy an important part of my being.

The constant inspiration for my writing is my honest critic, my best friend and the love of my life. She is the woman who said "I do" thirty-three years ago. When I am in my writing mode, I will scribble a few pages and then proceed to read them to her. She is my biggest fan, yet always honest with her feedback. This book is dedicated to my wife, Joy.

I am not a prolific writer. I go in spurts. Ideas for stories enter my mind on a regular basis, and occasionally one will stick. There is no preconception that I will ever be recognized as an accomplished author. I am not in this for fame and certainly not for fortune. It's just something I enjoy doing from time to time. We are all at different junctions on the road of life, and I am happy that you have decided to take a turn on "Pike's Path". Good reading to you.

1

The tiny pebbles crunched beneath his Wolverine boots as he walked across the rooftop of the warehouse. It was just shy of 6:00 A.M., and not a creature was stirring. Not even a spoiled little bitch ready to begin her busy day of bargain hunting. The soon-to-be-crowded parking lot was empty, with the exception of two-panel vans and a Honda Accord with a red towel hanging from the top of the driver's side window.

He pulled out his tin of Skoal and loaded up more than a pinch between his cheek and gum. Even after years of dipping, the cool wintergreen substance proven to cause mouth cancer still provided him with a pleasant, numbing buzz.

An empty five-gallon metal bucket served as his throne as he contemplated his months of preparation. The Remington rested across his strong, defined quadriceps. Soon, it would rest comfortably in his ready, steady hands. He knew that the formal clothing consignment store was about one hundred yards south of his command center, so he adjusted the rifle scope for that distance.

6:35 A.M. There was barely a cloud in the sky as he gazed out at the horizon. Humidity was low, and the high would be seventy-two. No chance of precipitation. No wind to affect any trajectories. Maybe he would get in a 10K run later in the afternoon.

    He spat out the wad of Skoal and rinsed his mouth with some Red Bull. The strawberry-filled Pop Tarts with sprinkled icing quieted his stomach growls. He laid the Remington across the bucket and surveyed the playing field. When the time was right, it would be his killing field. In just over two hours, the lot would be full of SUVs and minivans. Not today, but soon, it would be important for him to maintain his composure. Too much adrenaline could be a bad thing. It was now second nature to control his breathing. That hot-yoga DVD that he had watched and practiced time and again had been very helpful for his mental control. The heart monitor read sixty. Pretty good, but he wanted it at fifty-five. He methodically squeezed the rubber pump until the band around his left bicep was properly inflated. The descending numbers left him satisfied. One-fifteen over seventy.

    People would soon have to acknowledge his control and power. He would soon be in charge. He wouldn't be taking orders from anyone. He had meticulously designed and prepared for this mission. He had done the proper surveillance. He had trained his body. He had sharpened his senses. Preparation had been tedious, but nothing worthwhile could be achieved without proper discipline and organization. He would grade himself after the big day. That was important because he wanted to be accountable to himself, not any slacker teachers that had been peddling a bunch of bullshit to him for too many years. There would be five random targets. There would only be five rounds of ammunition available. Five fatalities would account for a perfect score. Anything under four would be a failure. Executing the kills was only part of the grand scheme. A fast yet controlled escape was oh so critical because there would be more missions to plan for in the future.

    The consignment store opened at 9:00. The lot was half

full by 8:30. Spoiled little bitches. Most of them had already shuffled off their spoiled little brats to school and daycare. Their charge cards would be on full tilt soon, and after they had bought a bunch of stuff that they didn't need, they'd meet their spoiled little bitch friends for lunch and pretend that they were enjoying their quiche and salad. A little later, they'd pick up their spoiled little brats from school and dump them at some after school activity. Or maybe some of them would keep their weekly appointment with their psychologist. They needed ongoing encouragement to deal with all the stress that life dealt out on a regular basis. They would compare notes on how effectively their counseling sessions were progressing. He thought about all the counseling sessions that he had endured over the years. Some with and some without his parents. What a waste of time. He sneered at the filling lot of luxury sedans and SUVs. Maybe more ammunition would be needed for the big day. He would really enjoy laying waste to some of the shiny new Beamers and Suburbans. He concentrated his sight on the scope as he surveyed the parking lot. An exhilarating rush came over him. A rush caused by an accumulation of anger and frustration that had built up over the years. He had learned to control these emotions, and fulfillment of his grand plan would allow him to release some of the energy. It was a beautiful day in the neighborhood, and he was in charge on this sunny October morning.

The aerator was barely a year old, but it had been a lemon since the day Billy Pike had purchased it. He strongly considered kicking it as it sputtered after each pull of the ignition cord. Yesterday, he had made a mental note to stop at the hardware store because he knew he needed a new gas filter and spark plug, but his wife, Paula, had texted him to pick up a few things at the Food Lion, and the aerator maintenance had completely disappeared from his mind. If Paula hadn't bothered him with her all-important grocery list, he would have tended to the aerator. Were any of the groceries so important that they couldn't have waited until she had time to go shopping?

"Piece of shit!" Billy cursed at the top of his lungs so the aerator could hear him.

Billy had to finish the job today because he had two big jobs staring him in the face for tomorrow. He climbed into his Ford F-250 and sped to Gunter's Hardware, and ninety minutes later, the aerator was humming right along. Billy rang the doorbell.

"All done, Ms. Howell."

"Hold on a minute. Let me fetch my purse." The old lady

handed Billy crumpled bills that totaled one hundred fifty dollars.

"Thanks, Ms. Howell. I'll see you next month for your fertilizer treatment. You take care."

Billy stuffed the cash in his bank bag and felt a small sense of satisfaction. This was a hundred and fifty bucks that good old Uncle Sam would never know about. The government had screwed Billy Pike more than once for this lifetime. Billy smiled as he thought, "Uncle can pucker up and kiss my ass!"

Billy stopped at Burly's Convenience store before heading home. A couple of cold Bud Lights were going to go down smoothly after this long day. Two little rug rats greeted Billy as he entered through the back door. The Lowells were late again in picking up Danielle and Curtis. At least three times a week, they were twenty minutes late picking up their bawling brats.

Billy unloaded on Paula. "You have got to be kidding me. Again? Those assholes are late again?"

"Billy! Watch your language around the children." Paula never got used to Billy's tirades.

"Watch my language. These kids don't understand what I'm saying. The Lowells are late all the time. I can't believe you don't charge them extra. Damn, Paula, they just keep taking advantage of you. Take up for yourself, and stop letting them walk all over you. Right is right, and wrong is wrong, and business is business."

Paula nodded but refused to prolong the rant. Not engaging her husband was usually the right decision. Hopefully, her husband would hit the showers and settle in for the evening. That was the usual ritual.

Paula watched four children from 8:00 to 5:30 every Monday through Friday. It was a strictly cash business, which suited

Billy just fine. More money that he would never report to his grand uncle in Washington, D.C. It was something that Paula felt guilty about in the early years, but she had stored her concerns away after enduring so many of Billy's monologues about how the government was out to screw the working man. She rationalized that keeping peace in her house was more important than tax rules.

The hot stream of water helped relax Billy's sore shoulders and upper back. After rinsing off and putting on his traditional gym shorts and T-shirt, he made his way to the kitchen and grabbed a Bud Light. He popped up from his recliner about five minutes later to get Bud Light number two. This one went down a little slower as he heard Paula and Loretta Lowell yakking in the living room.

"Oh, Paula. I'm so sorry to be running late, but a customer came in right at closing time, and I couldn't be rude to a customer."

Billy mumbled to himself, "I wouldn't think about pissing off a customer, but it's fine to shit on my wife all the time."

"Don't give it a second thought. Danielle and Curtis are no problem at all. Things happen." Paula's sincerity made Billy scratch his head in bewilderment.

Billy took a big gulp and headed to the fridge for number three. Loretta made sure that Danielle and Curtis gave Miss Paula a big hug before leaving, and Paula assured them she couldn't wait to see them again tomorrow.

The romance had started to fizzle out of their marriage a few years ago, but Billy and Paula still loved each other, and most of the time, their coexistence was civil. After beer number four, Billy called out to Paula, "I'm heading over to the Moose Lodge to shoot a couple of games of pool. I won't be late. I got a busy day tomorrow."

"That's great, Billy. It was so nice seeing you for five minutes today."

"Come on, Paula. Don't start in on me. What's the big deal?"

"No big deal, Billy. Nothing's ever a big deal to you. Do you ever think that I might need a break?"

"I'd invite you to come, but I already know you'll say no."

"That's right, Billy. I would say no. I mean, what woman wouldn't want to hang around with a bunch of fine gentlemen like the guys at the Moose Lodge? It's what I've been waiting to do all day. Drink beer and shoot pool with your buddies."

"Your sarcasm is out of line."

"That's funny, Billy. I'm out of line, but the idiots you choose to hang out with are not out of line."

"You know what, Paula? You always think you're better than everyone else. It's just a few guys hanging out after a hard workday to have a couple of beers and share a few laughs."

"Keep telling yourself that, Billy. You know and I know that you should avoid certain people."

"Certain people. Why can't you just say Hank Foster?"

Paula loathed Hank Foster and most of his cronies. She thought they were a bunch of ill-bred rednecks and hated the fact that Billy was spending more time with them over the past several months.

Billy made light of her concerns. "You are a constant worrier. Hank Foster's not the bogeyman."

Billy's reassurances rang hollow with Paula Pike. She was certain that Hank Foster and his buddies were dangerous men.

Billy Pike had known Hank Foster for as long as he could remember. Billy's dad and Hank served on the Board of Deacons at the Antioch Baptist Church. Hank had coached Billy a couple of years in Little League Baseball and had been a positive influence in his love of the sport, but Hank Foster had also made an early impression on Billy that was not so positive. Billy could remember the scene as if it had happened yesterday. It had been right after church service one Sunday morning, and Hank Foster and a few of the other Antioch brethren were talking about Lincoln Vernon. Lincoln had a tree-trimming and stump-removal business. He had a reputation as being an honest and hard worker. On one particular spring morning, Lincoln's assistant had notched a dead oak tree incorrectly. When the tree fell, there hadn't been enough time to warn Lincoln to get out of the way. Lincoln hadn't been bonded, and he hadn't had worker's compensation insurance. His surviving wife and five kids would have to find a way to struggle on without Lincoln. Hank Foster and the other men had bowed their heads as they seemed to lament the passing of Lincoln Vernon.

Billy's dad had driven the Ford Fairlane away from the

Antioch parking lot. The family was heading to the S&W Cafeteria for Sunday lunch. It was always S&W because that's what Billy's dad liked. His way or the highway. Billy's mom never complained. She was happy for her one-day vacation from the kitchen. Mr. Pike lit a cigarette and cracked the car window.

Billy had asked, "Hey, Dad. Is it ok for me to use the word 'nigger'?"

Mrs. Pike had jumped in before her husband could respond. "I don't know where you heard that word, but it is certainly not alright, and if I ever hear you utter that word again, I'll wash your mouth out with soap!"

Dad had held up a hand as if to signal his wife to calm down. "Well, Billy, your mama's right that it isn't a nice word, but how come you're asking?"

"I heard Mr. Foster use it a little while ago. He was talking about some man that just died."

"Billy, you've known Mr. Foster all your life. Hank's a good guy. I'm sure he didn't mean anything by it. Everybody except your mama uses a bad word every now and then."

Mama didn't return Daddy's sarcastic smile. The conversation was concluded.

Hank Foster was a disgruntled sixty-two-year-old man. For the past thirty-six years, he had worked as a claims adjuster in the worker's compensation department for the state of Virginia.

Just three months ago, Hank's supervisor, Lewis Morris, had called Hank into his office. "Hey, Hank. Have a seat. I guess you can guess why I've called you in here."

Hank had shrugged his shoulders in an aloof manner and defiantly asked, "Why don't you tell me, Mr. Morris?"

"Well, Hank, yesterday was the third time that you have been suspected of using alcohol during business hours. The first time was before I was your supervisor, and the second time was barely six months ago. There isn't going to be a chance for a fourth violation."

Hank had moved forward in his chair. "What the hell is that supposed to mean? I guess I'm guilty until proven innocent. Is that the way it is?"

"I'll cut through all the crap and give it to you straight. You can either hand in your resignation, effective immediately, or you can take the State of Virginia to court if you think you have a case. I'll expect a decision before you leave work today. This shouldn't come as a big surprise to you. I made myself perfectly clear when I disciplined you a few months ago. I'm more than happy to take some time right now to review your personnel record." Mr. Morris had cocked his head to one side and waited for a response.

Hank wasn't the brightest bulb in the pack, but he wasn't stupid. He knew his only option was to take the forced retirement because the agreement stated that he would retain his pension. There was no way a judge or jury would side with him. There was no telling what Mr. Morris had stashed away in Hank's personnel file. Spending a fortune for a lawyer on a weak case, at best, was out of the question. Defiant to the bitter end, Hank stood and stared daggers at his boss.

"I don't need until the end of the day. I'll give you my resignation on a roll of toilet paper, and you can wipe your ass with it. Thanks for nothing."

Hank Foster would spin the story in his favor. He was ready to retire and spend more time with family and friends. And just as important, devote more of his time and energy to the Patriots of America.

On multiple occasions, Hank Foster had approached Billy Pike about attending a meeting of the Patriots for America. A bunch of guys from the Moose Lodge were coming over to

Hank's house, and Hank thought Billy would enjoy coming over and spending some time with the fellows. They were having their weekly meeting and were open to considering new members. Billy was a member of the Lanexa Moose Lodge, and Hank promised him he would fit right in.

"You see, Billy, we got chapters all over the country. We got a bunch of good, law-abiding citizens who feel like their government is going in the wrong direction. Know what I mean?"

Billy nodded as Hank continued. "Us Patriots think that taxes are too damn high. You agree with that?"

"Sure thing. You'll get no argument from me on that."

"Exactly! The Patriots are sick and tired of all the lowlifes getting rewarded by the government for sitting on their asses and doing nothing. The government is handing out welfare checks like they're going out of style."

Billy kept nodding, and Hank kept talking.

"Now let me tell you another thing that really burns my ass. All this crap about protecting the rights of these flag-burners. My daddy and your daddy fought for this country. You think either one of them would say it's alright to burn Old Glory? Hell no!"

"And then there's that affirmative action bullshit. That ain't nothing more than a liberal plot to screw the White man. The Patriots love God, but the government must not. They're taking prayer out of all the schools. We're supposed to be a Christian nation!

"And then what about all of them illegals coming into our country. Most of 'em are in trouble with the law, and they're taking jobs away from real citizens. The damn army needs to set up on the borders and keep 'em out.

"And last but not least, the Patriots want to protect our second amendment. Billy, I know you like hunting with the boys. Well, if the government gets its way, you ain't gonna have your gun no more. They wanna take away our guns, and we say hell no! I'm telling you right now, you better buy as much ammo as you can before it's too late.

"All of this stuff is pretty much common sense to us Patriots. So, what do you think Billy? For your sake and your family's, I think you need to join our group."

Billy was less than excited about the invitation. It sounded like a political group, and Billy wasn't really into politics. "I'm not saying no, but I need to think about it some more. Not really sure I want to commit. By the time I get home from busting my ass all day, there's not a whole lot I feel like doing. But don't get me wrong. I agree with some of what you're saying. I promise you I'll think about it."

Hank Foster was a little put off by the rejection, but he made sure that Billy could rest assured that he would keep him "in the loop."

Billy wasn't sure he wanted to be in the loop, and he was certain that Paula would not even entertain any discussion that included Hank Foster. She had told Billy countless times that Hank Foster and his cronies were a bunch of ill-bred rednecks. Billy figured that the group was a harmless excuse to get together with buddies to tell tall tales and drink beer. He was certain that the Patriots were not a harmless group. God bless America.

4

Billy Pike actually kept his promise. He was home by 10:00. Paula was leaning on the arm of the couch, reading *Sense and Sensibility*. It had been a required reading when she was an English major at Virginia Commonwealth University. She remembered going to the campus bookstore and purchasing CliffsNotes for the novel that she hadn't read. Cliffs would give her a shot at passing the midterm, which she had with a B-minus.

Paula wanted the details from the all-important meeting at Hank Foster's. "So, please tell me what all important matters were discussed tonight."

"Really not much to tell. Just guys being guys. Hanging out. Shooting the shit."

"Sure, Billy. Thanks for sharing. I sit here all night while you hang out with Hank Foster and his kind. You come home and have nothing to share."

"Share? What do you want me to share? I told you it was no big deal."

"It's never a big deal with you, Billy. You come and go as you please, and you never have any time for your family."

"Never have time for my family! I come and go as I please?

You gotta be kidding me. What the hell do you think I do almost every day of the week? I'm out busting my ass for you all day long. You think what I do is easy? I ain't getting any younger, and I'm still out there every day putting up with more bullshit than you'll ever know."

"No one's saying you don't work hard, Billy. I appreciate all that you do. But Hank Foster? You don't need to be hanging with his kind."

"His kind? What is his kind? What makes you so high-and-mighty?"

Paula rolled her eyes and went back to her paperback. Over the years, she had tired of trying to extract information from Billy Pike. The exercise was exhausting. She knew that Billy would say he was tired and was going to bed and that they would talk about it more in the morning. But in the morning, Billy would say he was running late for an important job, and Paula would wish she was more important in her husband's life.

Billy's eyes welled with tears as he lay in the bed. He loved his wife, and he was disappointed in the man he had become over the past few years. In high school, Billy had excelled in baseball and football. Marie Bowman had been his sweetheart, and they were two of the most popular kids in school. There was no doubt that they would marry, have kids, and live happily ever after. The second half of their senior year made no doubt and happily ever after seem very uncertain. Billy had torn every ligament in his right knee due to a water-skiing accident, and Marie's heart had been captured by Kenny Thurston, one of Billy's best friends. Goodbye, happily ever after.

Billy's parents had enough money so he could go to college, but Billy would have to prove himself. The deal was that he would be expected to secure a part-time job for spending money and to help with other expenses. Billy could still recall his father's stern words:

"Your mama and I never went to college, but you feel like you need to, and that's fine by me, but you better understand something. This is gonna be on a trial basis. If I find out that you're just screwing off and wasting my money, I'll yank you out as quick as grease on a pig's ass. I've worked hard for my money, and I'm not gonna throw it down the drain for you to enjoy a great big party. Understand?"

Billy had understood, and it was no big deal. He had good work habits and a mature sense of responsibility.

Billy had enrolled at Virginia Commonwealth University. Freshman year was a real eye-opener. Billy had a full course load, a part-time job at Campus Pizza, and rehab appointments for his knee.

Sophomore year had been much better because that's when he met the love of his life, Paula Poynter. She and some friends had been sitting at a table one Friday night at Campus Pizza. After a couple of drafts and a medium pepperoni, her friends had been ready to party somewhere else. Paula had said she would catch up with them later as she had a few things to take care of. She had grabbed a stool at the bar and contemplated her strategy to meet Billy. A couple of hours had passed, and most of the crowd had filtered out.

Paula had approached Billy and gave him a piece of paper. "If you're smart enough to read, you'll see that I have written down my name and number. I'm sorry to be so forward, but I had no choice. You see, I've been hoping you would notice me for the past two hours, but I guess you've been preoccupied with more important matters."

Paula had promptly exited the pizza parlor, not giving Billy any chance to respond. Billy had called her the next day.

They had hit it off from the get-go and became inseparable. By senior year, they had been sharing an apartment in Richmond's Fan district. By the second semester, Paula had been pregnant, and three months after graduation, they were

Mr. and Mrs. Billy Pike. Hannah Elizabeth Pike had arrived in September, and Tracy William Pike had joined the family two years later.

Early memories of Paula, Hannah, and Trey helped Billy relax. The demands of his job and the distant relationship with his son caused a lot of stress in Billy's life. He harbored feelings of guilt concerning his lack of involvement in his son's life. He knew that he needed to be more caring to his wife. Tomorrow, he would talk to Paula and smooth things over. He would also think more about Hank Foster and the Patriots for Freedom.

5

Around 8:45 A.M., there were ten women standing in line, eagerly waiting for the front doors of Damon's Fine Fashions to open. Three of the customers had somehow coerced their husbands or significant others to tag along. What man didn't love spending his Saturday morning waiting in line to enter the aisles of bargains at Damon's Fine Fashions? Two of the women had babies in strollers. The other five were shopping solo. The men and the kids would be spared, but all of the bitches were fair game.

Five minutes later, eight more targets had joined the waiting game. He grinned to himself. The more, the merrier. Maybe I can nail two with one shot.

The sun was sitting high in the sky. The American flag hoisted at the building next to Damon's hung like a wet washcloth. He pumped the sleeve around his right bicep. This time, one-eighteen over seventy-two. Higher than he wanted, but nothing to be concerned about. Pulse was steady at sixty. Eager anticipation was so difficult to control. Next time, he'd be calmer and even more in control. He hoped this would never become boring.

Deep knee bends and some quad, hamstring, and calf

stretches helped him to loosen up. From shoulders to fingers, he shook his muscles and rotated his joints. He pointed his chin from shoulder to shoulder. Gotta stay loose. Don't wanna be tight when the moment is right.

Again, he focused his scope at the front door of Damon's. His dominant eye singled out someone who caused the hair on his neck to stand up. He instantly recognized the figure that was third in line. Raising his head, he wiped his eyes and then blinked. Squinting his right eye as he concentrated through the scope, he was not mistaken. Customer number three was Mrs. Walker. The same Mrs. Walker who was the mother of Leann Walker. The same Leann Walker he had dated in high school.

New Kent High's auditorium was the site for the annual Sadie Hawkins dance, which was held in March, just before spring break. The tradition was for the girls to ask the guys to the dance, and one day at lunch, Leann Walker had asked him to be her date to the dance. They had been in a couple of the same classes in junior and senior years, but they wouldn't have considered themselves to be close friends. He and Leann had barely been casual acquaintances. The invitation had been a complete surprise, catching him off guard. He had wanted to ask, "Why me?" but he hadn't wanted to draw attention to himself or embarrass her. He would pick her up at 7:00 next Saturday.

His mother had been thrilled at the possibility that her son might be starting some semblance of a social life, even if it was just one date. His father had no time for such trivial matters. Jack Daniels and coke had been much more important. He had assured his mother it was no big deal. Nothing he ever did was a big deal.

Even though there was a Food Lion and 7-Eleven less than five minutes from his house, he had driven ten minutes on 64 East and took the West Point exit. His fake ID had worked many times before at TR's Tackle Shop, and this occasion had been no different. He had put the Coors Light twelve-pack on ice in the styrofoam cooler and secured it in the back of his black pickup. The thought of popping one open had been tempting, but he might have to meet Leann's parents, so he had decided to wait. Nervously, he had rung the front doorbell, but he hadn't had to wait too long. Leann had greeted him. He had guessed it was her dad who yelled from another room to "make sure you're home by midnight." As they had walked to the truck, he had been sorry he hadn't had that beer.

They had made small talk about chemistry class, and both had agreed that the teacher, Mrs. Grinnell, was an asshole. He had listened as she talked about the softball team and Coach Herbert. She thought he was a pervert who wanted to get in the pants of most of the players on the team. He had taken her by surprise when he took a right on a dirt road just a few miles before the high school. Leann had tensed up when he stopped the truck and got out of the cab. She had been able to breathe again when he extended the Silver Bullet to her. She had lit a Marlboro Light; they had one more Coors and headed to the dance.

The deejay had played mostly rap and techno. Not his or Leann's favorite genres. After about ninety minutes, they had decided to find a more happening party. Her friend, Tara, had texted that her parents were gone until Sunday afternoon, so it made perfect sense to party at Tara's. There had been at least twenty cars when they got to Tara's house. He had known it was just a matter of time before someone called the cops. Leann had assured him that they would leave after a couple of beers. She had been true to her promise, and they had found their way back to their dirt road. Another couple of cold ones, and then Leann had pulled a joint out of her Marlboro soft pack. He wasn't shy about sharing, and within minutes, she had her Calvin Kleins below her knees and had been undoing his belt and lowering his zipper. Before she could get her lips around his tall soldier, the volcano had erupted. To make matters worse, she had begun to laugh, and the more frustrated he had become, the louder she had laughed. He had put the pickup in gear and peeled out onto the main road.

Leann had gathered herself and tried to take control of the situation at hand. "Chill out, man. It's no big deal. I'm sorry I laughed."

"Shut the fuck up. I don't want to talk about it."

Leann had made another attempt, but to no avail. How could he possibly face school on Monday? He had wanted to disappear as she approached him in the cafeteria.

She had said, "I promise you; it was no big deal. I really had a good time. Let's forget about it. I'm sorry I laughed. It's not the end of the world."

Leann had seemed sincere and had certainly been convincing. They had begun dating. It hadn't been a romance to be remembered, but they had some good times together until the evening of the prom. He and Leann and six friends had gone to dinner at the Cheesecake Factory and then driven to the school auditorium. The theme had been "Follow the Yellow Brick Road."

Leann and a couple of her friends had been talking. He had watched them intently and felt insecure as they all looked his way with smiles on their faces. The friend on her left had walked toward him. She had leaned into him and whispered in a sexy voice, "You might get lucky tonight. This time, don't be so quick on the trigger."

Leann had had no hope of stopping him as he had turned and jetted for the parking lot.

He gathered himself and looked through the rifle scope once more. Yes, that was definitely Mrs. Walker. That was definitely the mother of Leann Walker.

6

The three Advils had reduced the throbbing in his temples, but a dull pain lingered. Billy had long hours of aerating and mulching staring him in the face, and he didn't have the luxury of calling in sick. He filled the sink with cold water and buried his face. After repeating this a few times, he made his way to the kitchen, sipped on a black coffee, and was able to keep down a slice of peanut butter toast.

Billy conducted a supply check for the day's jobs and climbed into the cab of the Ford F-250. He wasn't in love with his work, but it paid the bills, he was his own boss, and most of his customers were willing to pay in cash. Between his business and Paula's babysitting, they were pulling in about $85K per year, and Billy was only reporting $35K to his favorite uncle. He kept a heavy-duty safe in the walk-in area of the master bedroom closet, which held nearly $50K in cash. Even Paula didn't know the combination.

Billy was the product of a blue-collar, middle-class family. His parents weren't poor, but Billy had never been spoiled with many luxuries growing up. Paula had attended private school from sixth grade through high school, so Billy liked to tease her, calling her a spoiled little brat on a frequent basis.

Most of the time, Paula let it roll off her back, but occasionally it irked her. Especially whenever Billy would go into one of his rants about the government "screwing the working man." Billy Pike felt like it was his prerogative. He had earned the right to voice his frustration. The government had screwed him. More than once.

This obsession had not always defined Billy. He hummed along to an Eagles song as he drove to the day's first job. The song brought back memories of college life. He and Paula had seen the Eagles in concert at the Richmond Coliseum twice while they were still students at VCU. Compared to now, those college days had been fun and mostly carefree. Even Paula's senior year pregnancy hadn't been a disappointment to either of them. They had welcomed it as a sensible reason to get married. Billy recalled when they were planning the wedding. "Paula, you got to be thinking about your dress. You know. The color. It can't be white. Only virgins can wear white." They would laugh and rarely argue about anything. Fun, carefree days. Where had they gone?

With his degree in criminal justice and hers in English, it made perfect sense that Billy went to work at the New Kent County post office and that Paula did office work for an insurance agency that was located in a strip mall close to their apartment in New Kent. The money hadn't been pouring in, but neither of them had been extravagant with their spending, and when Hannah was born in September of 1991, they had been filled with a love that couldn't be measured. Parenthood was a good thing, and as far as Billy was concerned, the sun would always rise and fall on his daughter.

Even though the postal job salary hadn't been great, the benefits had been excellent, and Billy had enjoyed off days for all the federal holidays. After being on the postal payroll for about eighteen months, Billy had received a bittersweet promotion to Postmaster. Roy Weaver had suffered a fatal heart attack, and even though he had lacked experience, Billy had been hired to fill the position. The pay bump had been substantial and really came in handy when Paula had given birth to their second child on April 6, 1994. Tracy William Pike was nearly three months premature. The Pikes had agonized for sixty-three days at St. Mary's Hospital. For the first three weeks in neonatal intensive care, there had never been a feeling of certainty that the baby would survive. Billy and Paula had known that they must carry on some semblance of normalcy for their daughter Hannah's sake, and that realization, combined with lots of faith and support from family and friends, had helped them through the draining ordeal. After a month, the ventilator hadn't been needed full-time. At the six-week point, in the words of the medical staff, the little boy had turned the corner and was beginning to thrive. Billy and Paula had counted their blessings. The anguish and stress that both had endured for those two months had been exhausting, and the fear that had gripped them had been paralyzing, but everyone had survived. This little boy would test his parents' survival skills again and again.

7

Hannah Pike was any parents' dream come true. Billy and Paula would never find a reason to commiserate with other parents when conversation was made about the terrible twos. That time in most mothers' and fathers' lives when they prayed for the strength to survive that cycle in the lives of their children. Hannah wasn't a crybaby. She wasn't needy. Hannah played well with her friends and was eager to share her toys. Hannah could entertain herself for hours. Hannah didn't throw temper tantrums. Hannah hadn't been jealous when her baby brother was brought home. At the age of three, she had wanted to mimic Paula and serve as Trey's second mother. Paula had beamed when her daughter told people that Trey was her baby. She would always be his protector and best friend. Hannah regularly assured her parents that there was nothing that Trey could do to make her stop loving him.

Hannah rode with her dad to Premier, which was a costume rental store in the Carytown section of Richmond. It was Billy's best bet to find a dinosaur costume. In June 1993, Steven Spielberg's *Jurassic Park* was released on the silver screen. When Trey Pike turned five, Paula and Billy had allowed him to watch the movie with Hannah. Trey was an instant fan of the rabid variety. It didn't take long for his bedroom to transform from purple Barney to Costa Rican jungle. Bed sheets, comforter, lamp, wall posters, action figures. Trey's bedroom was his dinosaur lair, and the ruler of the room was T-Rex. From the first vibration made by his gargantuan foot, Trey had been mesmerized by T-Rex. The other parts of the movie were ok, but it was T-Rex that was the star. At the age of three, Trey had a photographic recall of the movie.

Hannah clapped with excited approval as she watched her dad model the T-Rex costume. Eighty-nine dollars, and it had to be returned by noon the following day, or there would be a fifty-dollar late charge. Billy decided it was worth it. Hannah couldn't wait to see the look on her little brother's face when T-Rex raided his birthday bash.

Of course, the birthday party theme was *Jurassic Park*. Napkins, plates, dinosaur cake with a T-Rex figurine. Trey and his buddies loved it. With the exception of some video arcade tokens, every birthday present was associated with *Jurassic Park*. Paula placed the birthday cake on the patio table and herded the children outside. The happy birthday to Trey song ended. He successfully blew out the three candles. And then the earth stood silent and still. Hannah shrieked in terror as she ran by Trey and his troop. She had their attention. All eyes widened as the giant reptile lurched toward them. It was Tyrannosaurus Rex. He would destroy all little boys and girls in sight. His roar was deafening. The rampage continued for twenty minutes, and all the kids had miraculously survived. T-Rex was tired, but Paula assured them that after he ate, he would terrorize them again. It was the best birthday party Trey would ever have.

8

He didn't hold any malice toward Leann Walker's mother, but taking her out with his first shot would certainly cause pain and suffering for Leann, and that was something that she deserved. Leann had thought it was so funny when he had embarrassed himself on their first date. He had given her a chance at redemption, but she had betrayed him again at the prom. Leann had shared the details of their first date with her friends, and they had a good laugh at his expense. He didn't like being the comical figure. He felt anger and frustration and embarrassment. He wanted to punish her. Leann Walker deserved to be punished.

The building whose roof he occupied had once served as the main pottery center. It was built in the early 1970s, and the popularity of the place had spread like wildfire. Everyone called it the Pottery, but there were various craft shops and eateries as well. Getting in and out of the parking lots was a nightmare, especially on the weekends when customers would file in from as far away as Richmond and Virginia Beach.

His command center was now a storage building for pottery supplies. His recon over the past three months had proven that no one entered or left the building before early afternoon. There was one security camera near the loading door on the left side of the first floor. Deliveries and pickups were on Tuesdays and Thursdays. For the buying public, this building was a forgotten relic. Their attention was on the retail bargain shops.

Some of his dry runs had been acted out at nighttime. A three-foot-high cinder-block wall surrounded the perimeter of the rooftop. Getting to the top was what had presented the greatest challenge. In preparation for his practice runs, he had attached and secured climbing spikes every three feet from the ground to the rooftop. It was just a storage building. Who would ever take notice? He was in excellent condition. Well-defined muscles but not bulky. He ran forty miles per week at a six-and-a-half-minutes-per-mile pace. In addition to his free weights regimen, he gutted out two hundred sit-ups and two hundred pushups every day. Carrying the twenty-five-pound backpack up the wall was no struggle at all.

After reaching the top, he unzipped the backpack and assembled the Remington. He could do it in less than a minute and with his eyes closed if necessary. Sometimes, he would lie on his back and stare up into the sky. This was his territory. He was in charge. He was in control.

The front doors to Damon's Fine Wardrobes would be opening in just a couple of minutes. The back of Mrs. Walker's head was perfectly lined up in his sights. Now, there were more than twenty customers eagerly waiting to whip out their credit cards for the must-buys of the day. The first shot would be easy. His coordination would have to be perfect to deliver the next shots. Maybe the goal of five kills was too optimistic. It would be hard to control the adrenaline rush. He hadn't expected this worry to arise. He hated the fact that he was doubting his abilities. He needed to master his breathing and control his emotions. Closing his eyes, he took a deep breath and tried to reorganize his thoughts. He gained his composure and felt surer of the task at hand. The rifle felt good in his hands. There was no trembling. The time had arrived. His right index finger touched the trigger. Mrs. Walker's brains would be splattered on the sidewalk in seconds. And then there was a cold chill that paralyzed his entire body. There were voices just below his perch. He laid down the rifle and considered his options.

9

It was just after Labor Day when Trey Pike began kindergarten. It was a day that he was not looking forward to.

"But, Mom, I don't wanna go to school. I wanna stay home and play. I wanna be with you."

Paula had endured Trey's protests more times than she could remember. Thank God for her daughter. Hannah couldn't wait for school to start and had promised her parents that she would let Trey sit with her on the school bus and make sure that he got to the right classroom. Trey was nervous about his first day.

"I hate you, and I hate Daddy. You can't make me go to school. I hate everyone."

Hannah tried to help. "Trey, I didn't want to go to school my first day either, but it was great, and now I love it. Just think about all the new friends you'll make, and Mrs. Ferguson is so nice. She was my teacher, too. You will just love her."

"No, I won't. I'll hate her. I don't wanna go."

Billy had heard enough for one morning. "Hey, Trey. Cut the crap! And I mean now. You're going to school, and that's the end of the story. No one wants to hear any more of your whining. Not another word." Billy grabbed his lunch box and headed out for another long work day.

Standing her ground was tough, but Trey's tears wouldn't make Paula Pike cave in to the temptation of keeping him home until he felt more comfortable.

Mrs. Ferguson gave him a big hug when she welcomed him to her classroom. Trey's assigned desk was close to the teacher's desk, so that helped make him feel a bit safer. The atmosphere improved when several of his classmates thought his lunchbox was majorly cool. *Jurassic Park* featuring T-Rex.

That evening at the dinner table, Hannah was a Chatty Cathy on steroids. "This is going to be the best year ever! I love my teacher. She's so pretty. I'm in the best seat in the best row, and I've got great friends in my class from last year. Look at my books. They're all brand-new. The teacher wants me to have them covered by tomorrow. I want to get new book covers this time. No more crummy shopping bags. We have to go to Target tonight. I have my list of supplies right here. I think I'm definitely going to need a bigger backpack. When can we go to Target?"

Billy and Paula traded smiles to each other as they nodded their heads during the entirety of Hannah's monologue. She would never cause them one sleepless night. Their worry was Trey. He had made it through day one, but what would tomorrow hold? Billy was thrilled that Trey had gotten on the bus.

Week two was when the shit hit the fan. If Hannah was Chatty Cathy, then Trey was Silent Sam. Lots of times, she talked for her brother, and he never seemed to mind. Most of the reason was that he had a problem. Trey was a stutterer. It wasn't horrible, and Billy was certain that he would grow out of it when he started school.

Paula disagreed. "I think we need to meet with a speech therapist. Trey's different from Hannah. You see how he acts in the morning. I don't want the other kids to tease him. You know how cruel kids can be."

"Speech therapist! You got to be kidding. He doesn't need

a speech therapist. Give it a chance. A little more than a week in school, and you're ready for a speech therapist. Think, Paula. It's kindergarten, for crying out loud. Once again, you are overreacting."

Paula told herself that she was just trying to give her child the best chance that she could. But maybe Billy was right. Putting the issue on hold for now seemed reasonable.

Mrs. Ferguson announced to the class that it was time to learn more about the alphabet.

"Children, let's talk about the letter D. I'm going to say some words that begin with the letter D." She pointed to her desk. "This is my desk. The word 'desk' begins with the letter D. Some of you have a pet dog at home. 'Dog' begins with the letter D. If I use a shovel in my garden, I might have to dig a hole. The word 'dig' starts with the letter D. Desk, dog, and dig. All three of those words start with the letter D." The children nodded and understood. Mrs. Ferguson asked Trey to repeat the three words.

Reluctantly, Trey uttered, "Desk, dog, and d-d-dig." It was the third word that caused several classmates to giggle, but Craig Keely, in the row to Trey's left, was laughing out loud. Trey rose from his desk, moved toward Craig, and slapped him full force against the back of his head. Craig began to cry as Mrs. Ferguson moved quickly toward the two boys.

"Trey! Back to your seat this instant. I am surprised at you. We do not hit one another. Never. And Craig, we don't laugh at one another. That is not a nice thing to do. Now, I want you two boys to apologize to each other right now."

Trey thought differently. "No. You can't make me. He-he-he laughed at me."

There was some quiet giggling again as Trey buried his face in his arms on his desktop.

Billy and Paula received the phone call from Mrs. Ferguson that evening. They agreed to the suggestion that they meet with her the next day after school.

Mrs. Ferguson was stern but not dramatic. "Little arguments between children are to be expected, but I was surprised at Trey's tone and manner toward me. I am not a specialist, but I strongly suggest that you confer with the speech therapist in our school. Mrs. Banton has a wonderful rapport with children, and she has a fine reputation. Your son has some issues with his speech, and I believe it needs attention."

Paula appreciated the advice. "Yes, Mrs. Ferguson. I agree. "

The teacher continued. "Trey may also have a little problem with his temper. Have you noticed this at home?"

Billy jumped in. "I think all of us have a little temper, Mrs. Ferguson. I know I do."

"Yes, Mr. Pike, but maybe Trey hasn't learned how to control his."

Billy rolled his eyes and waited for the inevitable from his wife, who said, "Well, Mrs. Ferguson, I really thank you for bringing this to our attention. Billy and I will talk to Trey, and we will make an appointment with Mrs. Banton. Sooner than later."

Billy couldn't wait to leave the premises. He would reason things out with Paula and make her see that everything was getting blown out of proportion. Trey's just a little kid. Kids do stupid things sometimes. Trey would be fine.

Trey promised that he would be a good boy if his parents didn't take away his Nintendo for the next two weeks. He would tell Mrs. Ferguson that he was sorry, and he would even apologize to Craig Keely. Mom and Dad were willing to give their son a chance at redemption. It would be one of many.

10

It was a rarity for Billy Pike to miss a day of work, but on this particular Wednesday, he felt worse than awful, and he really didn't care if his customers would be sympathetic to his condition. He labored through the phone calls to the day's customers, explaining the situation, apologizing, and promising to get the work completed before Sunday. All except a new customer, Paul Grinstead, replied that they understood, that there was no problem, and that they hoped he felt better soon.

Old Man Grinstead was a pain in the ass. "You told me you'd be here bright and early. I got company coming in on Friday, and I want the yard to look nice."

Billy suppressed the urge to tell the old man to go screw himself. "I understand what I told you, Mr. Grinstead, but I just can't do it today. I promise you I'll get everything done before your guests arrive."

"Well, I guess I don't have much choice. Be here tomorrow, early."

"Yes, sir. I'll be there tomorrow."

Billy slammed down the receiver. He crawled back into bed and prayed that the chills would subside. Lots of fluids, lots of Advil, and lots of sleep. Hopefully, that would kick this bug in the butt.

Countless times, Paula had urged her husband to hire a helper. Landscaping was hard labor, and it would never get easier, and Billy wasn't getting any younger. Billy sometimes had a couple of high school kids from the neighborhood who wanted to make a few bucks on the weekends and during the summer, but he had never really sought out a full-timer since he had fired Leon Prince two years ago. Leon was a nice enough guy, and when he had shown up for work, he had worked like a mule. Showing up had usually been a question where Leon was concerned. Leon had an intimate relationship with his old buddy, Jim Beam, so there were many days that Leon had spent the good part of the day with his good brother Jim.

Billy thought back to his time working at the New Kent Post Office. He had accumulated thirty-seven sick days, six personal days, and three weeks of paid vacation. One of the main perks of the job had been the pension that would provide a decent income during Billy's retirement years. And if the government hadn't given him the shaft, Billy could still be working at the post office and could have used a couple of those thirty-seven sick days, and he wouldn't have to be wasting his time explaining to Old Man Grinstead that he felt like shit and wouldn't be mulching his freaking yard today.

In the late 1990s, the voters of New Kent County had gone to the polls to vote yea or nay on an annexation referendum. The official tally had been "yea" by a slim margin. The voters had agreed that it was in their best interest to be annexed by the nearby city of Williamsburg. Even though their real estate taxes would increase, they had been assured that it would be a small price to pay for being recipients of better municipal services, which would be provided by the government offices in Williamsburg. Offering high-speed internet at a discounted rate for the citizens of New Kent would be a top priority. Less expensive trash pick-up and a new service for recycling would be available. Razing the forty-year-old New Kent Elementary and building a shiny new one with all the latest bells and whistles would be given serious attention. And oh, by the way, you would be able to be proud and proclaim that you lived in one of the most historic cities in the world. A city that was a sought-out destination by travelers all around the globe. That's right. You will live in Williamsburg!

Shortly after the annexation, the powers that be had decided to streamline the postal operation. It would make more sense to centralize all services in Williamsburg. March 31, 2001, had been Billy Pike's last day with the postal service. They had been sorry, but his position had been a necessary budget cut. They had hoped he understood, and just to prove their commitment to doing what was fair, they had given Billy ninety days of severance pay. They had been sorry that they couldn't compensate him for the accumulated sick days, but they would pay his health insurance premiums for the month of April. And the pension. Billy could start taking seventy-eight dollars per month when he turned fifty-five, or he could take a lump sum for a little more than three thousand dollars. That's what Billy Pike was worth after ten years of loyal service.

Billy hadn't even considered filling out forms to collect unemployment. He had been fortunate enough to find a job at Barksdale Paper Corporation in nearby King William County in the little town of West Point. The company had employed about five hundred workers, and its biggest customer had been the federal government. Billy had spent the first thirty days in training, learning how to work in the assembly line for packaging. The new position certainly hadn't been his dream job come true, but the benefits were good, and you could almost always get overtime hours if so desired. Billy had known several of the employees. A lot of them lived in New Kent, and a few of them were in his hunt club. There were some that he remembered seeing at Hank Foster's meeting of the Patriots for Freedom.

After two years at Barksdale Paper, Billy Pike had become a casualty of corporate downsizing. The federal government hadn't renewed its contract with Barksdale. Management had had to cut nearly twenty percent of its staff, and Billy's lack of seniority had put him in that twenty percent. Being low man on the totem pole hadn't been as hard to swallow as the postal dismissal had been, but once again, Billy had felt that he had been screwed by the government.

It was early afternoon and time for more Advil. Billy groaned as he rolled out of bed and made his way toward the kitchen.

Paula intercepted him. "Billy, what are you doing? Get back to bed. Now. If you're hungry, I'll bring you a grilled cheese and some chicken noodle soup."

"That sounds good. I appreciate it."

Billy could hear the voices of Danielle and Curtis Lowell from the den. He popped a couple of Advils and thanked his God above that he didn't have Paula's job.

11

Throughout all the rehearsals, he had never seen one person near his building. Today was the exception. On the ground stood two men. They were passing conversation as they leaned against their work van. Neither seemed to have a care in the world as they sipped coffee from large styrofoam cups and regularly puffed on their cigarettes. Pretty early in the day for a break, but with no supervisor around, the mice will play. He could hear them talking but couldn't make out the specifics. The big blue letters on the van spelled out Finley's Heating and Air Conditioning. He glanced to his left and focused on the large air conditioning unit on his rooftop. Maybe he could fire two quick rounds and be rid of these guys in short order. The possibility was tempting. Disassembling the rifle and descending to the ground before anyone noticed could be accomplished, but it was a risk he wasn't willing to take. His heart rate was steadily increasing as random thoughts raced through his cluttered mind. Mere seconds had rendered him out of control. Breathing was too rapid. Throat was dry. Hands were trembling. Body felt limp. Slow down the breathing. Gather yourself. The Finley guys were lighting up another cancer stick. No telling how long these guys would be here. Time to move. He carefully made contact with each spike as he made his way to the ground. He was angry. Angry with himself that his grand scheme had been disrupted. But angrier with himself that he had lost his focus. He was not in control. There was new work to be done. Someone had once told him that patience was a virtue. Maybe so. Mrs. Walker's brains would stay intact this day.

12

There was a M*A*S*H* marathon on one of the thirty-four cable stations, and semi-coherently, Billy Pike was binging season two. Parents had picked up their kids, and Paula went to check in on her ailing husband.

"Hey, Billy. Feeling any better?"

"Yeah. I think I'm going to live."

"I'm going out for a run. Need anything before I go?"

"Nah. Be careful."

"I shouldn't have to ask, but I hope there's no chance that you're going to Hank Foster's later."

"No, Paula. Nothing to worry about."

"Ok. I'll check on you when I get back."

Lacing up her Nikes, Paula thought she would get in an easy three miles. Paula had grown up the youngest of four. Her three brothers had served as her protectors. All were jocks and knew how to handle themselves if the need ever arose. Paula had dated very little in high school. It had been a blessing and a curse that most of the boys wouldn't ask her out because they were afraid of her brothers. They had been the reason that she was drawn to athletics. Every weekend had been dominated by some type of sport. From kindergarten through high school, her parents were always in attendance for her brother's games. And that's the way it always had been. Paula had played soccer, basketball, and softball, and she had yearned for her parents' attention, but her participation had always seemed to be an afterthought. She usually had felt like the runner-up.

It was in middle school that she had found her niche. Cross-country running. Maybe it had been her subconscious that found the inner drive to achieve something on her own. Maybe it had been an acclamation of individuality. Whatever it was, it had been her thing. Her specialty had become the sixteen-hundred meters. Paula had been the district champion in her junior and senior years. She had run the anchor for the sixteen-hundred-meter relay team that finished second in the State of Virginia in her senior year. A partial track scholarship had been awarded to her by Virginia Commonwealth University. She had performed well at the college meets, but she had known she wasn't destined to run in the Olympics. By sophomore year, the grind of a full academic workload and track practice had become a job. Running hadn't been as enjoyable as it had been in high school. She had wanted to enjoy other aspects of her college experience, so she had decided to forgo track after her second year.

Paula never regretted that decision as she found that running as a hobby was much more fun. It served as a form of stress relief and her method of meditation. She thanked God that she could escape from time to time. Between her husband and her son, it was a miracle that she wasn't in therapy. Billy's involvement with Hank Foster's group was a growing concern. Billy's lack of involvement in their son's life was a heartbreaker. It was a relationship that had been deteriorating for years.

In the elementary years, Billy had always been insistent that Trey would grow out of his stuttering and behavioral problems. He had dismissed Paula's warnings that little problems would lead to bigger problems. After countless teacher conferences and reprimands, by the start of middle school, Paula Pike had drawn her line in the sand. She had said she was going to file for divorce if Billy didn't agree to professional help for Trey. Billy had assured her that the professionals were in cahoots with big Pharma. She could remember Billy's warnings as if he had spoken them yesterday.

"Go ahead and do what you've wanted to do since he was in kindergarten. Take him to some weirdo psychiatrist who will diagnose him with this problem and that problem. And then he'll tell us Trey needs to be on this drug and that drug, and before you know it, he'll be walking around like some zombie drug addict."

Paula couldn't lie to herself. She had shared some of Billy's concerns, but she knew their methods had been unsuccessful. "Well, Billy, we've been trying it your way for a few years now. Can you honestly tell me that you think Trey's behavior has been improving? I'm tired of going along with everything you want. I love my son, and I think he needs help that you and I can't provide."

"Your son? Now he's your son?"

"Pretty much accurate, considering how involved you are in his life."

Those words had hurt because Billy had known they were mostly true.

"Go ahead, Paula. Do whatever you want to do. When he's screwed up even worse than now, don't come crying to me. Because I'm going to remember this conversation, and I'm going to tell you I told you so."

"Of course you will, Billy. I fully expect it."

"So, what are you planning to do?"

"I'll get some references and set a meeting with some kind of counselor who specializes in kids Trey's age. I really think it might be helpful. Do you think I don't want what's best for

Trey? I don't want to wake up five years from now, kicking myself for not doing something earlier."

"Well, if you're hell-bent on this thing, then both of us should go with him to the first appointment. I'll be damned if I'm going to let Trey loose, one-on-one with some shrink. No telling what kind of bullshit either one of them might say."

It was a rarity for Paula Pike to win a battle against Billy. She was proud of herself that she had stood her ground.

Paula had made the necessary arrangements for weekly meetings, and they hadn't been as horrible as Billy had expected. He had been amazed that the doctor wasn't a total weirdo and relieved that he wasn't a drug pusher. Dr. Frank was all about communication. He could teach the family effective communication skills, and most of their issues could be handled effectively if certain methods were practiced every day.

Trey loved his parents. Trey loved his sister, Hannah. Trey didn't love himself, and he didn't think his dad loved him. Trey could never measure up to Hannah. She had lots of friends and a charming personality. Trey was a loner and an introvert. Hannah made straight A's. Trey struggled to eke out passing grades. Hannah was a cheerleader, played softball, and ran track. Trey went through the motions as a member of the middle school football team. Hannah was Daddy's pet. Trey had to get counseling to try to get along with Daddy.

Paula had broken a nice sweat. She kicked up her pace as she made her way back to the house. As she stretched in the driveway, she hoped that Billy was feeling better so he could go to work tomorrow. Not for his sake, but for hers.

13

When Billy Pike lost his job at Barksdale's in 2003, he had made up his mind that he would never put himself in that position again. He would be his own boss and make his own work rules. Billy had never learned a trade, but he wasn't afraid of work. Even hard work. He had inherited that strong blue-collar work ethic from his parents and knew that Paula and the kids were his responsibilities, and he would only apply for unemployment as a last resort. There were plenty of neighborhoods throughout Williamsburg and an abundance of retirees and golf courses. It was a popular destination for retirees. Lots of Northern state transplants made Williamsburg their home. The climate was more desirable, and it was much more affordable than living in New York and Connecticut. And they took great pride in the upkeep of their homes. Especially their yards.

Pike's Home Services could satisfy all your year-round landscaping needs. Power washing and snow removal were also offered. Paula had created a colorful flyer from her laptop, taken it to Kinko's, and made five hundred copies. She and Billy had distributed the flyers throughout a couple of suburban developments near the Golden Horseshoe Golf Club. It hadn't taken long for his phone to ring a few times. One referral had led to another, and Pike's Home Services had been off and running. The hours were long, but the business was his. The equipment was his. The work schedule was his. Billy Pike was the boss of Billy Pike. And very importantly, the money was Billy Pike's. Many customers didn't mind paying in cash. More for Billy and less for Uncle Sam. The government could kiss his ass.

Darrell Taney and Jeb Johnson were two of Billy's hunting buddies. The three amigos met for beers nearly every Friday afternoon at the Buck and Bass, a good-ole-boy bar and grill not far from the Pottery Factory in Williamsburg. It was 2006, and on this particular Friday, Darrell Taney was monopolizing the conversation. With each Budweiser, Darrell got a little bit louder and even more obnoxious. CNN was reporting that there had been a stampede in Saudi Arabia, resulting in the deaths of three hundred sixty-two Muslims.

"Three hundred sixty-two is a good start, but a thousand would be better." Darrell thought he was a real comedian.

CNN reported that Iran had refused to allow United Nations inspectors to analyze their nuclear capabilities. Darrell's solution: "Stop asking and just bomb the hell out of the whole damn country. Shoulda done it after we got the hostages back."

Saddam Hussein would be sentenced to death for crimes against humanity. More commentary from Darrell: "It's a shame some of our boys couldn't have taken that bastard out years ago."

Following Darrell's international insights, his conversation with Billy and Jeb turned to television.

"Either of you guys watch 24? Well, I can tell you this. That's the best damn show there is. That Jack Bauer is a true badass, and if anyone don't like that show, they're an idiot. If we had some more Jack Bauers in charge, this country wouldn't be so screwed up."

Billy rolled his eyes and laughed out loud. "Hey, dumbass.

It's just Hollywood. Not real. You realize that, right?"

"No shit, Sherlock. I'm just saying. Oh, forget it. Either one of you guys watch that faggot show, *Queer Eye for the Straight Guy*? If you do, you ought to be ashamed of yourself. I told my old lady to never turn on that shit in my house."

Billy couldn't resist saying, "Maybe you should start your own show and call it *Straight Eye for the Queer Guy*."

Jeb spit out his beer as he roared with laughter. Darrell failed to see the humor.

Billy finished off his long neck. "Gotta go. See you guys next time. And Darrell, don't forget about nine o'clock."

Darrell had a puzzled look on his face as Billy clarified, "Nine o'clock. That's when *Queer Eye* comes on."

After several invitations from Hank Foster and some of the other Patriots, Billy Pike had decided to join the ranks of the Patriots for Freedom. Since that decision, Paula Pike had been feeling her husband drift further away from her and the kids. Any social life that she shared with Billy revolved around friends of his who were also members of the Patriots. Every other Saturday night, it was off to the local Moose Lodge for dinner, dancing, and booze. Paula was conflicted. She still loved her husband, and he worked hard to support the family, and she wanted him to have some fun times with his friends. But these weren't her friends, and she had nothing in common with the men, their wives, or their significant others. Paula had never discussed it with Billy, but resigned herself to leave him once the kids were grown. She had tried countless times to reason with her husband about too many subjects to count. Paula wanted to be included in the family's financial decisions. Billy managed all the income and expenses. He even collected Paula's daycare income. There had been several times when Billy shot down her suggestions about their social lives. He didn't want to go to dinner or the movies with any of her friends. They were all a bunch of liberal weirdos. She thought he needed to spend more time with Trey and Hannah, and that was something he was always going to do but never did.

Hank Foster called the meeting to order. A quorum was confirmed, and the minutes from the last meeting were read by the secretary. Following approval of the minutes, the only old business to discuss was membership dues and the new project.

Hank Foster had the floor. "I hate to even bring it up, but we're going to have to raise dues a little bit to help pay for the new project. You all know we've been kicking this can down the road for a while now, but we can't be kicking it anymore."

Most of the Patriots agreed to the dues increase and were excited about the new project.

Patriot member Dean Glass was recognized by Hank Foster. "It's way past time for the project. We should have started on it months ago. Y'all all know that. Everyone knows the country ain't like it was when we were growing up. It's gone to hell in a handbasket. Ever since Reagan left office, things ain't been the same. Those damn Clintons were crooks and worse than the Mafia. George W's been trying to fight the good fight, but he can't get nothing done because of all those liberal Democrats. They shoot him down every single time."

All heads were nodding as Dean continued. "Now, this election coming up is going to be a close one. We got to get out in force for John McCain. That guy's a real war hero."

Hank Foster thanked Dean Glass for his words and continued. "Dean is right. We need to be united in November. Get everyone in your family, get everyone in your church, get everyone you know to get out and vote for McCain. Can you imagine what'll happen to this country if that liberal Obama wins? I don't think anybody but the liberals and the Blacks are going to vote for him, but we can't be too sure. Can you imagine a Black man in the White House? God forbid! But if he does manage to win, it makes our new project even more important."

Billy Pike took all this in. Billy wasn't into politics. Heck, he hadn't even voted since Reagan's first term. He wasn't as gung-ho as some of his fellow Patriots seemed to be. Truth be told, a few of them made him a little bit uncomfortable. They seemed pretty rabid about certain issues, especially race relations and the Second Amendment. He would never let his wife know his thoughts, but maybe she was right about Hank Foster and the Patriots. For now, Billy would pay his dues and just try to fit in.

14

Trey Pike was sorry that the summer was coming to a close. For the first time in his life, he felt like he was a part of something. His life had some purpose. Larry Drummond was one of Billy Pike's Patriot buddies. Larry owned a residential construction company and had a good reputation for building high-quality custom homes. As a favor to Billy, Larry had hired Trey for the summer and weekends when school began. Trey didn't have any work experience, so in the early going, he was just a gofer, but after a few weeks, Larry discovered that Trey possessed some acumen in carpentry. Larry was so pleased that he had someone who showed up for work when they were expected. Billy and Paula were cautiously optimistic that their son may have found a profession that would employ him after high school.

Sophomore and junior year grades were barely passing, and Trey's only academic objective was to graduate on time. What he really wanted was his own transportation. Paula had wanted Billy to cosign a loan for a used pickup at the end of the last school year, but Billy adamantly refused until Trey was willing to get a job for the summer and save enough money to pay toward the purchase. Working for Larry Drummond had allowed Trey to save about three thousand dollars, and Billy reluctantly agreed to match that amount for the black Toyota Tacoma that Trey purchased from a nearby used car lot.

Billy warned Trey, "You know the deal. You pay half of the insurance on the truck, and you pay for your own gas."

Trey understood.

Billy continued. "This is a big responsibility. It's not a toy, and you are not allowed to let any of your friends drive it. And absolutely no drinking and driving. If you screw this up, I'll confiscate the vehicle until further notice. Understood?"

His father really had a way of ruining the excitement, but Trey said he understood.

Larry Drummond called quitting time on this particular Saturday afternoon. After pulling down the tailgate on his Dodge Ram, he pulled the Coleman cooler toward him, opened the top, and pulled out two Coors Lights.

Glancing at Trey, he said, "I know you're not legal age to drink, but I'm sure this ain't your first beer. Now, don't say anything to your parents because I don't want to hear a bunch of shit about contributing to the delinquency of a minor. A couple of beers ain't going to hurt anything. Hell, if you're old enough to do an honest day's work, then I say you're old enough to have a beer."

Trey liked Larry's philosophy and couldn't have agreed more as he popped the top.

"Ya know, Trey, this is a big year for you. You'll be graduating soon, and you'll be able to vote next year. Ya know you got to register to be able to vote."

"I don't think I'm too interested in that. I don't really keep up with that kinda stuff."

This news lit a fire under Larry Drummond. "Don't care about it! You better damn well start caring. You and all of your young people better start caring something about it. You got any idea what all of them liberal Democrats are trying to do?"

Trey shook his head.

"I know you like to hunt. Right?"

Trey nodded as he took a long sip.

"Well, they want to take our guns away. Just because there are some whackos out there shooting up schools and shopping malls, they think everyone with a gun is a nut case. Didn't they teach you anything in school about the Second Amendment?"

"I'm not the greatest student, Mr. Drummond. I think we're learning something about it in government class."

"Well, you better listen up in class because it gives every citizen the right to own a gun. We need this to be able to protect our homes. You know anything about this Obama guy?"

"Not really. I mean, I know a little bit."

"Well, he and his kind are bound and determined to do away with the Second Amendment and confiscate our guns."

"No, I hadn't heard anything about that."

"You better open up your damn ears and pay attention. If you think I'm full of shit, ask your old man. Ask your old Little League coach, Hank Foster. They'll tell you what I'm saying is right."

Larry collected himself and took a long swig of his beer. Trey thanked him for the cold one and made his way home. Larry had always been straight with him. Maybe he really knew what he was talking about.

15

He returned later in the afternoon to find not just one but two Finley's Heating and Air Conditioning work vans. One man was on the roof, while the other three were enjoying another nicotine fix. He stopped to wonder if Mr. Finley had any idea how much money these employees were costing him. A couple of the warehouse workers joined Finley's finest for a smoke break. Maybe they all would break out a cooler and order a couple of pizzas because there sure wasn't an ounce of work effort being exerted by anyone on the ground.

His plans were ruined for the day. Maybe he could regroup and start anew tomorrow morning. He knew that Sunday was the second busiest day of the week at the outlets. The targets would be plentiful. A long flatbed tractor-trailer approached the warehouse. Trailing it was a Chevy Suburban and a Ford Explorer. Seven new bodies joined the Finley party. The new guys unloaded a heavy-duty crane from the flatbed.

It became apparent that this was going to be a lengthy operation. They were going to replace the rooftop air conditioning unit. Most likely, they'd be working on Sunday. Heck, with this bunch of sloths, the job might take the whole week.

He cursed his bad luck as he disappeared into the woods. Throughout all his planning, he had realized that there were factors that were out of his control. This was just a minor setback. A temporary interruption. He would use it as an opportunity to refocus. Patience was a virtue. He had never considered himself a virtuous man.

16

The Sportsman Hunt Club was situated on seventy-five acres of woodlands owned by Spottswood Construction Company. Spottswood Construction's CEO was Bayne T. Spottswood, III. Junior and Senior were still active in the business, although Senior's workdays mainly consisted of reading the sports, comics, and obituaries and popping his head into people's offices to see how their families were doing.

Senior was affectionately known around the office as the "Old Man." Junior was B2, and appropriately, his son was B3. B2 had formed the hunt club in the 1970s, and he promised the Old Man that he would be sure to control the membership. That meant family, close friends, and loyal long-time customers. Billy Pike's dad had been a project manager for forty years for Spottswood and had enjoyed being a part of the club. He had suffered a massive heart attack on a Monday morning at his work desk. Billy had inherited his membership in the Sportsman Club. Sometimes, on special occasions, he'd bring Trey along.

B2's wife was the sister of Hank Foster, so naturally, the president of the Patriots for Freedom was in the Club. As a matter of fact, there were several Patriots counted among the membership. Annual dues were $1000 per member, and B2 collected all of it in cash. Everyone's fat Uncle Sam would never sniff one cent of the fat cache.

Deer season was popular in New Kent County. Hunting was ingrained in the culture. There were even some women engaged in the sport. Archery season ran from early October to mid-November. There was an early muzzleloader season in November and a late one in mid-December. There was regular shotgun season, which was the most popular. There were too many acres of public and private hunting grounds to count throughout the county.

Rules and regulations regarding deer hunting were abundant, and the Spottswood family made sure its membership followed them. B2 didn't want undue attention to his property. If you ever crossed the line, there was no reprimand; you automatically forfeited your right to even hunt on Spottswood land again. No exceptions. Trey Pike learned this when he was seventeen.

Trey and a couple of his buddies were caught on a Saturday night. They had parked their truck outside the gate at the Hunt Club. B3 and his wife had finished dinner at a local restaurant, and he needed to swing by the club to pick up a couple of files.

He told his wife, "Just wait in the car. This'll only take a minute." B3 saw a truck parked several yards away from the gate. He picked up the clubhouse phone and immediately called his father. "Hey, Dad. I had to run by the club for a minute. There's a truck parked near the gate. I'm not sure who it belongs to."

"Stay where you are. I'm on the way."

Cautiously, B3 walked outside, straining his eyes in the direction of the parked truck. He could hear voices. Louder with each passing second. Then he heard someone exclaim, "Oh shit! Someone's coming. Let's get the hell outta here."

But it was too late. B2 had arrived and was shining a

heavy-duty signal light in the direction of the truck. He yelled out, "Whoever is out there better get their asses to the gate, and I mean now!"

A young man walked slowly toward the light. B2 was flabbergasted. "Trey Pike? Is that you?"

"Yes, sir, Mr. Spottswood."

"Who else is with you? They better show themselves right now."

"No one else, Mr. Spottswood. Just me."

"I know that's a lie. This isn't your truck. What the hell are you doing here? You know this place is off-limits after sundown. Now, one more time. What the hell are you doing here?"

B2 listened to Trey's story as he drove him home. You could have heard a pin hit the floor when B2 escorted Trey into his house. The looks on Billy's and Paula's faces represented utter confusion.

B2 said, "Evening, Billy, Paula. I'll trust Trey to tell you what happened tonight. Sorry to disturb your evening."

Trey recounted the evening's events to his parents. It didn't take long for Billy to explode.

"You have got to be shitting me! Spotlighting deer? Who else was with you?"

"I'm not telling on my friends."

"Not telling? Oh, you don't need to tell. I can pretty much guess who it was. A couple of dumbasses just like you. You know the rules about the Spottswood land. Did you ever stop for one minute to think how dangerous it is? Firing live ammunition at night. You're damn lucky no one got hurt."

"Can I just go to my room now?" This was not the right question for Trey to ask.

"I'll let you know when you can go to your damn room! So, let me get this straight. You're guilty of trespassing. You're guilty of spotlighting deer. Y'all were probably drinking. Am I right?"

Trey shook his head.

"Your grandfather worked his whole life for Old Man Spottswood. Your grandfather was one of the first members of the Sportsman Club. I remember how excited I was when my dad took me to the club for the first time, and I've been a proud member for a long time. I remember taking you when we gave you your first shotgun for your fifteenth birthday. And now look where we are. You'll never be allowed to step foot on those grounds again, and I will look like a dumbass in front of all my friends. I can't believe you are such a selfish prick!"

Paula tried to intervene. "Billy. Try to calm down. Don't say things you don't mean. I think Trey knows—"

"You think Trey knows what, Paula? Trey obviously doesn't know shit! If he did, we wouldn't be having this conversation right now. Would we?"

"Billy, I know you're upset, and you have every right to be upset. I'm upset and disappointed, too. It's not always just about you, Billy. I just think it would be better to discuss this more in the—"

"Discuss this more in the morning. Is that what you were going to say? Guess what? In the morning, I'm still going to be pissed, and our brilliant son is still going to be a ..."

Billy was able to catch himself, but Trey could fill in the blank. Dumbass. Loser. Disappointment.

Hannah removed her headphones and hurried to the den. "Jeezy, Dad. You're yelling loud enough for the neighbors to hear you. What is wrong?"

"Go ahead, Trey. Why don't you tell your sister why I'm yelling so loud to wake the dead? Do you think Hannah would ever do anything as stupid as this?"

Trey knew the answer, as did his mom and sister. He withdrew to his bedroom and tried to absorb the hurt that he was feeling. Hurt that he was responsible for but hurt nonetheless. Some of the hurt would never subside. He knew he was a disappointment to everyone, especially his father.

17

Trey Pike sat in his U.S. Government class listening to Mr. Farrell drone on about the checks and balances system of the three branches of the federal government. Why in the world did he need to know about this crap? Trey was going to build custom homes with Larry Drummond. If it wasn't for his mom, he'd be on the job right now. But she was always there for him. Paula defended Trey even when he didn't deserve a defense. She was ever ready to praise her son for the most trivial achievement. If for no other reason, he owed it to her to get his high school diploma.

As Mr. Farrell lectured on presidential veto power, Trey's thoughts were on Friday's home football game. Last season, he had played sparingly, but he would be starting linebacker this year. It was the same position that his dad had played in high school. As excited and nervous as he was about having a starting position, he was more concerned about not being a disappointment to his dad. The tension seemed to always be present between father and son. Trey recalled the birthday party when Dad had dressed up as T-Rex. He remembered riding dirt bikes with his dad one summer. It had been such a big deal the first time Billy let Trey hunt with him at the club. These memories could make Trey smile, but these memories were far too few. Trey recalled so many conferences with teachers. The outcomes all seemed the same. Trey had a difficult time controlling his emotions, or Trey didn't follow instructions, or Trey was not prepared for class, or Trey was caught smoking outside the gym, or Trey was spotlighting deer, and Trey was a major disappointment to his father. These past and recent events shaped the main part of Trey's self-image.

New Kent won the home opener on Friday night. Trey Pike had four solo tackles and recovered a fumble. His most special reward was hearing "great game" from his dad. Maybe football would serve as the filler to the hole in Trey's relationship with Billy. It was certainly awesome to hear congratulations from his coach, and he welcomed compliments from teachers and classmates the following Monday at school. Trey was hesitant to see a light at the end of the tunnel, but he was feeling better about life and, more importantly, about himself than he could ever remember. Could he possibly make the hands of time stand still for just a little while longer? Trey Pike knew the answer to that, and it dimmed the possibility of light at the end of that tunnel. The bad thoughts always outshone the good ones.

Trey thought back to driver's education class in the tenth grade. He remembered the early mornings of behind-the-wheel instruction from Coach Glass. He remembered his mom driving him to the DMV to test for his driver's permit. A test that he had had no confidence in passing. Trey had never performed well on written tests. His middle school counselor, Mrs. Evans, had informed his parents that Trey suffered from dyslexia and needed to have regular meetings with a specialist. The past four years had shown little improvement. But by a minor miracle, Trey had passed the test, and he had been proud to get his license. But what good was the license? He, Dylan Day, and Randy Peterson had made the brilliant decision to spotlight deer on the Spottswood property, and now

Trey's truck had been confiscated by his father. What a joke, and what a waste of time.

Trey closed his eyes and remembered Hootie Herman's party. Trey and Hootie had hunted together because Trey's dad and Hootie's dad had always hunted together. It had been January of Trey's sophomore year at New Kent High. Hootie's parents would be away for the weekend to do some skiing at Wintergreen Resort. It had been the perfect opportunity to have a few friends over for a Friday night party. Trey had assured Mom and Dad he would be home by midnight. He and Hootie were just going to grab a pizza and play some video games. Word of a party usually spreads like a California wildfire whenever teenagers are involved. Hootie never knew he had so many friends. The get-together of a controllable few had steamrolled into a rager for the ages. Two cruisers of Williamsburg's finest had made their presence known at Hootie's house. There had been at least fifty teenagers that ran like cats being chased by Rottweilers. When the smoke settled and the dust cleared, Trey and Hootie were the two left to face the fire.

Trey Pike wasn't going to the juvenile detention center for the underage drinking conviction, but maybe it wasn't such a terrible option compared to the punishment being handed down at Pike's Penitentiary. Trey would serve time for the next month, and if he complained too much about the severity, Billy would be happy to add another thirty days to Trey's sentence.

Trey recalled the ride home after the cops had busted Hootie's party. Billy had been irate. "It was the middle of the night, and your mother and I get a call from the cops that our son is being charged with possession of alcohol and we gotta come pick his dumb ass up at the Williamsburg Government Center, and he was supposed to be eating pizza and playing Nintendo, and we can't believe a damn thing our son ever tells us, and this is just one more stupid ass thing that you have done in your stupid fucking life, and we don't give a rat's ass if everybody else was drinking, and we don't give a shit that a bunch of other dumbasses got away but you got caught because you deserved to get caught for being a liar."

The five-minute rant had felt like an hour.

The days that passed had been pretty mundane for Trey. It wouldn't be time concentrated on studying or improving his grades. Texting and television would serve as his main courses. Paula's heart went out to her son, but she had decided she wasn't going to intervene concerning the punishment even though she felt it was two weeks too long.

On the first Friday of Trey's grounding, Billy and Paula had told him they'd be home around 10:00. They'd be at the Moose Lodge. He recalled his parents' warning, "Stay put and don't do anything stupid."

Trey had his license. He could jump in the truck and be home by 9:30. Who would ever know? What good was it to have your driver's license if you never had a chance to use it? He had shifted into reverse and backed out of the driveway. The truck had idled in front of the house. Trey had two texts.

One had been from Greg Gordon. "Me and some buddies are going to take our four-wheelers onto the seventh green at the rich boys' country club. Meet us at my house around 10:00."

The other text had been from his mom. "Just checking in to see if you are ok. See you by 10:00. Love Mom."

Trey had slammed the shifter into drive and ascended the driveway.

The ringing of the bell that marked the end of Mr. Farrell's class startled Trey. Leaving high school in his rear-view mirror couldn't happen soon enough.

18

The crime scene was like something from a bloody horror movie. Half of the man's head was plastered against the stair railing. The high-caliber bullet had reduced the woman's face to a skull full of mush. The daughter's hands were manacled behind her back. Duct tape was bound to keep her ankles together, and a large strip was mashed down across her mouth. Her clear blue eyes pleaded with the monster to spare her life. He offered an eerie grin to her as he waved the serrated dagger in front of her face. Tears streamed from her eyes as he unzipped his jeans. He felt such empowerment. Control was his favorite aphrodisiac. He moved toward the middle of the room and programmed the incendiary device for ten minutes. There wouldn't be any mistakes he would need to worry about. The authorities could sift through the bones and the ashes, but they would never link him to the crime. If he ever became bored with his conquests, then maybe he'd leave a clue here and there to make it more of a challenge. Five minutes to go. He savagely tore the tape away from her mouth and dared her to scream. Her pathetic pleadings only made him feel more invincible. He exited through the back door and reveled in Leann's torture.

The satisfying ejaculation woke him from his sleep. He needed to concentrate on his new game plan. Last night's dream was certainly an inspiration. He scouted out the warehouse near the Pottery Factory for the next three days. Finley's Heating and Air Conditioning had finally replaced the big roof unit. On Thursday, there were no signs of any workers. He would give it a few more days to make sure the job was completed. On Monday, the coast was still clear of any activity at the warehouse. Saturday would be the day. This time, there wouldn't be any interruptions. He would be in control.

19

The new project was going to be built on Spottswood land, not far from the Sportsman Hunt Club. The plans called for target practice areas for bows as well as shotguns. The plans detailed an indoor shooting range, too. A large underground ammo bunker would be dug just behind the Hunt Club's lodge. There would be a supply building that would hold non-perishable items and an industrial-sized freezer for storage. This would be phase one.

Bayne Spottswood, Jr. (B2), envisioned emergency housing, above ground and below, for phase two. The Spottswoods were one of the wealthiest families in Virginia. The Old Man had made political connections in his younger years, and the family influence was substantial at the local as well as state governmental levels. The Spottswoods thrived on political intel, and they were privy to lucrative construction plans before they were ever made public.

Big amounts of Spottswood money went to support local law enforcement, firefighters, and various first responder units. The Spottswoods aggressively supported conservative politicians at the local, state, and national levels, especially those that aligned themselves with the Religious Right.

The new project would be built by Spottswood employees, who would supervise each and every phase. Delays from local and state departments would be minimal because these agencies were in the Spottswoods' deep pockets. Building permits and inspections could bring any construction project to a snail's pace. Spottswood money bought a lot of advantages.

It was a lively, boisterous, profanity-laced meeting of the Patriots for Freedom. No voice was louder than Hank Foster's.

"How in God's name have the people of the United States of America voted a Black man into the White House? Who in the hell ever heard of Barack Obama before the last few months? What has he ever accomplished? He ain't nothing but a neighborhood organizer from the crooked city of Chicago. Here's a guy with no experience, and he beat the shit out of a real American hero, John McCain. You got to be shitting me! Most people don't even think he was born in this country. His father's from somewhere in Africa."

The Patriots were nodding in agreement as one yelled out, "His damn wife is a racist. She hates White people."

Hank Foster continued. "So, what's going to happen now? Well, I can guarantee every one of you that your taxes are going to go sky-high. It won't be long before they'll be coming for your guns. Hell, it won't be long before the White man is the damn minority in this country. Lemme tell you boys something. This here is a wake-up call. This is a sign. This is a call to action for people that really love their country."

Most of the Patriots agreed with Hank. He had fired them up into a frenzy. The call to action meant full steam ahead on phase one of the project. B2 added that time was of the essence. The Patriots needed to act while the Spottswoods still held some clout in the area.

B2 thought the timing was right to rededicate the members to the principles on which the Patriots were organized. Hank Foster agreed and read them proud and loud:

- A Patriot believes first and foremost in Freedom.
- A Patriot fully supports the Second Amendment of the Constitution.
- A Patriot supports and has membership in the NRA.
- A Patriot believes that Jesus Christ is the only way to God.
- A Patriot believes that homosexuality is a sin against God.
- A Patriot protects and defends the United States flag.
- A Patriot believes in the sanctity of life and condemns abortion.
- A Patriot will protect his family from any threat, foreign or domestic.
- A Patriot will defend a fellow Patriot.

There was clapping and cheering at the end of each testament.

B2 addressed the Patriots. "We're only a small cog in the big machine, but you can rest assured that we have brothers of the same mind all over this great country. Brothers that live the principles that you just heard from Hank. We are gaining momentum. There's a bunch of good folks that agree with us. They'll join in once they see some of our progress. We're going to help take this country back from all the liberal socialists that have been dragging it down for years. We're not going to sit on our hands. We ain't going to play the fiddle while our country is burning down. We're going to be heard before it's too late."

Billy Pike had been pretty quiet for the duration of the meeting. It was easy to get swept up in the emotion of the moment. He found himself nodding in agreement to some of the remarks, but there were some principles that he questioned. He didn't know much about Obama, but he didn't have any hangup that the new president was Black. Billy's mother had always taught him that prejudice was based on fear and ignorance. Billy thought abortion was justified in certain situations and believed that the decision should be in the hands of the mother, not some governing body. Paula had an uncle that was gay, and Billy had never had a problem with him. Billy was in lockstep with the Patriots on the other principles, and he rationalized that no group was perfect. These Patriots were far from perfect.

20

Billy Pike had not lived a life that was full of traumatic events. He was the only child of Junius and Clarice Pike. His family was blue-collar and middle-class, through and through. Billy had gotten along well with his parents, but he certainly hadn't been a spoiled kid. Pikes were put on this earth to work. Junius' philosophy was hammered into Billy from an early age. At the age of ten, he managed a neighborhood paper route. Every morning, rain or shine, Billy had pedaled his bike, delivering the morning news. Every Thursday, he had gone door to door, collecting money for each week's subscription. By the age of twelve, Billy had retired from the newspaper business and moved on to self-employment. Cutting grass. In addition to his own yard, he had managed the lawns of six other houses in and around his neighborhood.

Junius and Clarice had surprised Billy with a car on his sixteenth birthday. It had been a 1964 Chevrolet Bel Air that had a faded teal blue paint job and bumpers that were starting to rust, but as Junius had loved to proclaim, "the engine ran like a top." Billy had been thrilled to have his own transportation. It would be his responsibility to pay for his gas and half of the insurance. Billy couldn't count the number of times that friends had piled into that old Bel Air. Good times.

His family had loved the great outdoors and owned a double wide that they kept near the York River, just south of Williamsburg. Every weekend during the summer was spent at the river. Billy had usually been allowed to bring a friend along, and they had enjoyed dirt bikes, fishing, and simply hanging out with all of the other kids from the trailer community. The weekends had never been long enough for Billy and his friends.

No one had called Billy's dad Junius. He was Juny to young and old. Juny had enjoyed his Jack and ginger ale, especially on the weekends. This had gone hand in hand with his two-packs-a-day habit of Marlboro Reds. Juny was only forty when he had suffered the first heart attack. Billy had only been fifteen. This should have served as a wake-up call for Juny. His doctor had advised him to cut out the cancer sticks and to cut back on the brown water. Juny had switched to Marlboro Lights and cut back to one pack a day, but Juny had truly believed that life was too short to not be able to enjoy it. The second attack at age forty-eight had led to double bypass surgery, and after this, Juny had never struck another match. Juny never recovered from number three at age sixty.

Spottswood Construction was the only employer Juny had ever known. Billy remembered the strong work ethic inherent in his father. The Spottswoods had treated Juny like one of the family, and Billy had always looked forward to the annual Fourth of July cookout and annual Christmas party at Old Man Spottswood's estate. Billy had continued the traditions into his college years and, by that time, was allowed to enjoy a cold beer with the men folk. Billy could picture them as they puffed their cigars and addressed all of the problems of the day.

A smile appeared on Billy's face as he recalled one July Fourth. Old Man Spottswood had sat in a rocker on the broad side porch of the main house. The stogie in his left hand had served as his baton as his right hand clenched his Jack on the rocks.

"The country is going down the shitter. The White man is an endangered species. The liberals have taken Jesus and the Ten Commandments out of the school. The younger generation didn't have any respect for their elders. All these illegals coming into the country are taking away good jobs from hard-working Americans. And these illegals are getting free health care and ain't paying any taxes. That's why my taxes are so damn high. And what in the hell is the government spending all our tax money on? I'll tell you what they're spending it on. A bunch of horse-shit programs that pay folks not to work. That's right. In this country, you can sit on your ass and collect a paycheck. It sure as hell wasn't that way when I was growing up."

Old Man Spottswood had rested the back of his head on the back of the rocker. He'd be napping soon. At his age, he had been no match for a stiff bourbon. Old Man Spottswood had drifted off to sleep while his audience continued discussing some of the topics that had been presented.

All those years ago, Billy Pike hadn't had a serious care in the world. Billy had been content to leave the problems of the day, as well as their possible solutions, to Old Man Spottswood and his cronies. But today was different. The Patriots had their list of grievances. Hank Foster and the Spottswood clan weren't just making conversation on the wide porch on the side of the house. Yes, today was quite different. Billy Pike wasn't smiling anymore.

21

He balanced his right foot on the metal spike and began his climb to the rooftop. The only light that shone was from the neon store lights in the distance. The parking lots were empty except for a few company vans. He would patiently bide his time until sunrise and then concentrate his attention on coordinates and distance. A slight easterly breeze wouldn't cause any problems. The line outside of Damon's Fine Wardrobes would start to form around 8:30, so he had more than two hours to concentrate on the mission at hand.

Closing his eyes, he assembled the rifle. Disassembly followed, and then he repeated the steps. Controlled breathing was essential. He knew it would be difficult to harness the adrenaline after the shots began. He was one with the weapon. No more practice putting it together and breaking it down was necessary. Concentration on the mission needed to be his primary focus. All the weeks of patience, practice, and preparation would soon be rewarded.

He noticed two Williamsburg Police cruisers that had parked in front of Damon's. A quiet morning had allowed the officers to blow off a little time to shoot the shit. They would have no reason to move toward his warehouse, and after twenty minutes, they had driven out of sight.

Staring at the cop cars had allowed his mind to drift to his run-ins with law enforcement. None had been very serious, and he'd never served any jail time, but he had definitely made life difficult for his family.

Much to his father's chagrin, his mother usually heaped the blame on others. "He's really not a bad kid. He just needs focus. He's hanging out with the wrong crowd."

Dear old Dad wasn't buying Mom's defense. "Always excuses. You're always blaming someone or something else. He's responsible for his own behavior. No one's holding a gun to his head when he makes bad decisions."

He was usually content to watch from the sidelines as his parents analyzed him. He realized that his dad had been kind of prophetic, with the exception of where he would be pointing the gun.

He tore away the foil from the Pop-Tarts and scarfed down breakfast. The Red Bull provided a nice little kick as he surveyed the parking lots. No activity and about an hour to go.

Concentration was an effort, and he couldn't get his father off his mind. He had always wanted to please him, but just didn't know how. The learning disability that school specialists had diagnosed was more serious than his parents ever believed. He had known he was different from the other kids, and this had caused him to embrace paranoia. It had caused him to lash out at teachers and fellow students. Demerits and detention had been commonplace from middle through high school.

He remembered one particular counselor's words to his parents. "Your son is starved for attention."

He entertained the words in his mind. Maybe so. Definitely so. The time was drawing near for the fulfillment of that need. He felt that his parents wanted him to be like other kids. Normal kids. The other kids knew who the kids who received special education were. And kids could be cruel.

How many counselors had spoken these words to his parents? "He has difficulty staying on task." "He does not work well with others." "His reading comprehension is below his peers." "He has low self-esteem."

The Ritalin was supposed to be a wonder drug, but it had made him feel anxious and caused nausea and headaches. He'd forgotten the names of wonder drugs number two and number three, but both had caused irritability and aggression. The doctors had always strung his parents along by promising, "You need to be patient. It takes time to find the right combination for the prescriptions. Everyone is different."

Yes, everyone was different, especially him. He had found his most efficient drug combination by the time he entered high school. Pot and alcohol. Unfortunately, he hadn't been very efficient in regulating the dosages of either, and both had put him in trouble with Williamsburg's finest and his parents on multiple occasions. Suicide had been contemplated more than once, but the welfare of his mother had always stopped him.

Thirty minutes until target time, and he wasn't focused on the mission before him. A handful of cars were parked outside of Damon's, and the sky was gray. The controlled nervousness was absent. Anticipation and excitement were nowhere to be found. He felt an unnerving mix of anxiety and sadness. For a moment, he considered placing the rifle barrel in his mouth. He was not in control. He had always been a disappointment to his father. Even though she would never admit it, he was a disappointment to his mother as well. He was a disappointment to himself. His hands were shaking as he disassembled the rifle. His legs felt heavy as he descended the wall.

22

October 16, 1995, had drawn attendees, most of them Black men, to Washington, D.C. They had traveled from all over the country to listen to more than twelve hours of speeches calling on Black men to take responsibility for improving themselves, their families, and their communities. Nation of Islam leader, Louis Farrakhan, had spoken for more than two hours, detailing the role of White supremacy in the country's suffering while urging Black men to clean up their lives and become better fathers, husbands, and neighbors. Farrakhan had blasted the White establishment. The gathering had been the Million Man March.

Farrakhan and other African American leaders were organizing another rally to be held in Washington, D.C., for the summer of 2012. The theme would be Justice or Else. Leaders of Black Lives Matter, the group that arose in response to police-related deaths of Black men, would have prominent organizational authority for this high-profile gathering. Civil rights leader, Benjamin Chavis, noted that an Illinois senator had attended the Million Man March, and that senator was well on his way to becoming the next President of the United States. Obama was leading McCain in most public opinion polls, and it was rumored that Obama would speak at the rally.

This was a bitter pill for the Patriots for Freedom to swallow, so they decided to organize their own trip to the nation's capital. The Spottswoods were going all out to fire up the troops. B2 and B3 had custom Winnebago Horizons to transport Patriots for the northward journey up Route 95. They had reserved a bus that could seat another eighty Patriots and friends. The goal was to hook up with ten thousand more Patriots from other chapters around the country. Reports on patriotsforfreedom.org and various social media outlets assured that the Patriots would be well represented in the nation's capital. The Patriots wanted to take advantage of this opportunity to air their agenda for others to hear.

Billy Pike worked overtime in the two weeks leading up to the rally in order to be able to attend. The Spottswoods and Hank Foster had urged all members to make this a family event.

Half-heartedly, Billy tried to recruit Paula, but he knew it was a waste of time. "You need to try to see the big picture here. The Patriots are trying to bring attention to some issues that are important for the future of our country. I'm doing this for my family. For our future."

"You got to be kidding me, Billy. When did you become so fired up about the political future of our country? You're listening to the wrong people. Hank Foster and his kind are a bunch of ignorant racists."

"You don't know what you're talking about. For whatever reason, you have never liked Hank Foster, and that's your choice, but 'racist' is a little strong."

"Well, what would you call him?"

Hannah chimed in with her opinion. "Come on, Dad. Mr. Foster is a racist. So are most of your friends."

"You don't know what you're talking about, little girl. Just because you've completed a couple of years of college doesn't make you an authority. What has Mr. Foster ever done to you or Trey? You shouldn't just listen to your mom and all her socialist friends."

"Socialist friends? Billy, it's not worth discussing this anymore when you make such ignorant comments."

"Yeah, Paula. I'm ignorant. Maybe you're afraid to learn something that might just help your family one day."

"Billy, the smartest thing you can do is not go on this trip to D.C. You're asking for trouble."

"No, Paula. You're the one asking for trouble by just being content to sit by while your country goes to hell in a handbasket."

Trey decided to observe the fireworks. He had never been passionate about much of anything, so it was surprising when he entered the conversation. "I'll go with you, Dad."

Paula immediately objected. "No, you won't. Not while I still have my wits about me. Your father is a grown man and sometimes capable of making his own decisions. But you are my son, and I will be responsible for protecting you."

Billy shot back. "Per usual, you are exaggerating the situation. You make it sound like it's a life-threatening adventure."

"If you think for one minute I'm going to let my son go with you and a bunch of radical rednecks who are going to meet up with another bunch of radical rednecks, then you are sadly mistaken."

"This is going to be a peaceful demonstration. You make it sound like it's going to be the shootout at the OK Corral. You should be happy that there are enough concerned citizens about all the crap that is being shoved down their throats by that liberal crew in D.C."

"Right, Billy. I'm thrilled. I'm sure you and Hank Foster and the Spottswood clan can save our country from all the evil forces that are trying to destroy it. This is just so weird. It's so unlike you. Where is all this sudden passion coming from?"

"So, I'm not capable of being passionate about something?

Am I just a caveman?"

Hannah thought the question was pretty funny. "Well, yeah, Dad. You are kind of a caveman."

The arguing shifted back to Trey's welfare.

"He's my son too, Paula, and I'm saying he can decide for himself. You can't keep him under your wing forever. He's eighteen, for God's sake."

"Come on, Mom. It's not that big of a deal."

"Trey, I love you, but you don't understand the danger of this situation. There will be thousands of people. Your father is wrong in advertising this as a peaceful gathering. It's a powder keg waiting to explode."

"Mr. Drummond's going. He's been talking to me about some of the stuff that his and Dad's club believe in. What's the harm in me going?"

Paula was on the verge of tears and didn't want to lose her emotional control. "I'm not discussing this anymore. Billy, you know how I feel. I'm so disappointed in you. Not for your decision to go but for not dissuading Trey from going. I know that you would never have considered this trip if you hadn't gotten involved with these Patriots for Freedom. You should be ashamed of yourself."

Paula stormed out of the room and retreated to her bedroom. The slam of the door shook the house.

23

On the eve of the trip to Washington, Paula Pike tossed and turned in her queen-sized bed. The argument with Billy and Trey had really upset her. She had always tried to honor her mother's wise advice: "Never go to bed angry with one of your loved ones." Paula was tiring of the growing number of disagreements with Billy. More and more distance was being created, and Paula feared that one day she would wake up and just not care any longer. Billy's acceptance of including Trey befuddled her. She was certain that Billy was using their son as a pawn to spite her.

Just as she was beginning to nod off, Paula could hear Billy and Trey stirring around. It was 4:00 A.M., and they were getting an early start to venture up Route 95 for the big Patriot rally. It was all so surreal to her. How had it come to this? She wiped tears from her eyes as she heard Billy's truck leave the driveway. Maybe she was being overly dramatic, but she couldn't control the terrible thoughts that raced through her mind. Her husband and son might never return home. There were so many things that could go wrong at the demonstration. It was ridiculous to think that security could control the crowds that would be gathered. Washington, D.C., was hosting the twentieth anniversary of the Million Man March, and thousands of the Patriots for Freedom would be in attendance. What could possibly go wrong? This was nothing more than a racial clash being instigated by the Patriots for Freedom. What dumbass had issued a permit for the Patriots to gather? How had it come to this? How was half of her family involved in this? These questions were torturing Paula Pike.

All the challenges Paula and Billy had faced with Trey had taken its toll on their marriage. Billy's affiliation with the Patriots had been casual at the onset, but over the last few months, his involvement had taken a defined direction. She felt like her husband was bordering on obsession with certain topics such as taxes, gun control, and immigration. Paula's politics had always leaned to the left, and Billy's had opposed hers. Billy's rants against the liberal agenda were waged on a regular basis and with greater intensity.

Paula thought about the bitter argument she and Billy had had a few days ago. It was still vivid in her memory.

"Jeez, Billy. I can't believe that a person of even average intelligence believes that this country doesn't need better gun control laws."

"I guess you're complimenting me with average intelligence. I appreciate that and am relieved that you and the rest of your liberal friends are well above average in the brains department. That's just what we need. More laws. Do you have any idea how many gun control laws there are now? You think they are helping in any way?"

"You believe people should be allowed to buy assault rifles? Just tell me, Billy: Who needs an assault rifle?"

"Personally, I don't need one, but I'm not going to stop someone from buying one."

"Every one of these school massacres. Assault rifles."

"Damn, Paula, it's not the assault rifles. It's the crazy people with the assault rifles."

"And if there weren't any assault rifles, the loss of lives wouldn't be so dramatic."

"You hit the nail on the head. Dramatic. That's your media for you. They're always exaggerating everything. The media is trying to control you."

"I think twenty-seven dead children is pretty dramatic, Billy."

"Let me assure you of one thing. If the gun lobby ever caved in to your kind, it would spell disaster for every law-abiding gun owner in this country. The next thing they come after is your handgun and your shotgun, and pretty soon, they'll be taking the Second Amendment out of the Constitution."

"God, if that doesn't sound like one of the most paranoid comments I've ever heard in my life. You sound like one of those radicals out in Idaho. A bit dramatic, don't you think?"

Neither Paula nor Billy would concede any ground. Like most of these encounters, it ended with no middle-ground resolution. They would fight it out another day.

It was impossible for Paula to exorcise her demons of guilt. She had a habit of blaming herself once the dust settled and the smoke cleared. There were too many what-ifs for her to count. Should she have been more supportive and sympathetic to Billy when he had suffered two job layoffs? Should she have secured a full-time job to ease any financial concerns? Should she have sided more often with Billy where Trey was concerned? Could she have tolerated Billy's friends more convincingly? Had she used the divorce threat too many times? There were even more questions where her son was concerned. And now, as Paula lay in her bed, she thought about what the day had in store for Billy and Trey. None of the possibilities were encouraging. Some of them caused her to shake with fear.

Traffic was a nightmare, so as Billy and Trey approached Northern Virginia, they decided to park in Arlington and take the Metro into D.C. For the first time in either of their lives, they knew what it felt like to be in the minority. At the turnstiles and in the subway cars, there were twenty Blacks for every one White. Trey was uneasy and tried to persuade his dad to head back home, but Billy was determined to rendezvous with his fellow Patriots.

Billy made a half-hearted attempt to reassure his son. "Settle down, Trey. Everything's going to be fine. Nobody wants any violence. Just stay close to me. We'll be alright."

His father's assurance didn't convince him.

The Patriots' gathering spot was supposed to be at the Washington Monument. It was a sobering sight to see the numbers of law enforcement officers equipped with shields and tear gas. Some were on horseback, and there were a couple of canine units. As the father and son neared the Monument, they witnessed an engagement that was drawing a lot of attention from all within hearing range. A twangy voice shouted into the microphone. The sound was amplified through the stacked, concert-size speakers. At least one hundred Knights of the Ku Klux Klan were gathered on and around the stage, and they applauded their leader as he addressed the massive crowd. "Our once great country is at a crossroads. The men and women that built this country are being reduced to second-class citizens. The government is helping the Black man at the expense of the White man."

The hissing and booing volume was much greater than the applause, but nevertheless, the Klansman continued.

"The government is giving away our jobs to all the illegals coming in from Mexico. We need to let our leaders know that we aren't going to sit by and continue to take this abuse. Ever since our great brotherhood began way back in 1865, we've been working to save this country from the demons within. And here we are today, standing our ground against the scourge that is threatening our very existence."

Hundreds of Black men pressed toward the stage. They didn't need a microphone. Pushing and shoving with Klansmen was scattered. Verbal clashes were rabid, and the volume was escalating. The intensity was at a fever pitch. Violence could erupt at any second. Just one nervous cop could blow the top off this pressure cooker.

"Get off the stage. Hillbilly bastards! Nobody wants to hear your racist bullshit! Go back home!"

This prompted a chant, "Go back home. Go back home. Go back home."

Trey wondered how he and his father would ever get out alive. Trey wanted to run to the nearest Metro station, but he couldn't take his eyes off the stage. Billy interrupted the mesmerizing moment and grabbed his son by the shoulder.

"Let's get the hell out of here while we can. This isn't what I was expecting. Not by a long shot. I haven't seen a single Patriot. This is the Klan. Where the hell are the Patriots?"

It was the first time Trey had ever seen fear in his father's eyes. Billy's pulse was racing. He was scared, and he was angry. Angry with himself for putting his son and himself in harm's way.

"Hey, Trey. Let's head back toward the Metro and get away from all these people."

They found a Chinese restaurant and settled into a booth. Billy remembered the first time he had ever been to the nation's capital. It had been a field trip in the seventh grade. He remembered visiting the Smithsonian and the Lincoln Memorial. On another occasion, his dad had taken him to a Redskins football game at the old RFK stadium. Today was Trey's first father-son trip to D.C. A chance to meet up with Dad's Patriot brothers, who would detail their plan for saving the country.

Billy closed his eyes and felt ashamed. He began to question his abilities as a father. Hannah was any parent's dream child. It had been easy to raise her. She had always been so eager to please everyone around her. Trey had been a challenge from the very start of life. Bringing him into the world had been wrought with risks to mother and child. Billy recalled the weeks of uncertainty as his little boy had lain in an incubator. The emotional stress on mother and father had been suffocating. Trey's emotional issues had contributed to so many road bumps in school. Billy knew he should have been more active and hands-on with Trey's development. But he hadn't been. Billy had been satisfied to kick the can down the road. It had been fine with him for Paula to manage every crisis. Rationalizing every situation had become easier and easier. Billy was too busy with work, or some other excuse would always cover his shortcomings as a parent. Billy couldn't blame his parents. They had taught him to prioritize his responsibilities, which included "family first."

As Billy looked across the table at Trey, he sincerely felt ashamed that he had put his son in harm's way. And for what purpose? To attend a rally for the Patriots for Freedom. To win an argument with his wife, whom he knew had been right in her objections.

Billy and Trey ordered food. When the check arrived, Billy cracked open his fortune cookie and read it to his son: "I am a dumbass, and I hope you will forgive me."

It was the best that Billy could come up with now. It turned out to be the perfect line to ease the tension both were feeling. Trey laughed and shrugged it off. "Don't worry about it, Dad. Let's just get outta here. I want to go home."

Billy nodded in agreement and hoped he could find his way back to his family. He knew it would be a difficult road, but he was willing to take the first step.

24

For too many years to count, New Kent had been the doormat of the league in high school football. The final game of the regular season was approaching, and if the Trojans could find a way to win, a spot in the state class-A playoffs would be secured. Since his run-in with the Spottswoods, Trey Pike had mostly stayed on the straight and narrow. His demons were usually present, but Trey had been able to keep them at bay for the past few months. The recent encounter with his father had given Trey some emotional strength. He longed for his dad's approval.

Fortunately, Trey and his teammates would have the support of the home crowd for the all-important game. The Trojan faithful was out in full force. Standing room only. The atmosphere was electric. New Kent scored two touchdowns in the first quarter and never looked back. The Trojans were going to the playoffs for the first time in seventeen years. Gatorade substituted for champagne in the raucous locker room following the victory. Coach Glass awarded the game ball to the entire team and urged every player to get plenty of rest over the weekend and be ready to go hard at practice on Monday. The coach's words seemed to make good sense that Friday night, but a lot of players had forgotten their coach's advice by Saturday. Besides, the season had been a grind. The players had toiled through the hot, humid summer practices and had rewarded the community with a great season and a trip to the playoffs. Certainly, a modest celebration was not an outrageous expectation. The party would be at Julie James' house. Go Trojans.

Over the summer and throughout the fall, Paula and Billy Pike had noticed a change in their son. Trey was more responsive. He wasn't a member of the National Honor Society, but he was passing all his classes. None of his teachers had requested conferences, and he hadn't accumulated any demerits. Maybe he was maturing and being a bit more responsible. Maybe the discipline from football had carried over into other aspects of Trey's life. He was still working weekends with Larry Drummond and saving a little bit of money. Trey had always ignored the lectures concerning time management and goal setting, but he was managing his time better, probably out of necessity, and he actually had a couple of goals in sight: Graduate from high school and start his own company building custom homes. He would continue to work with and learn from Larry until he had the confidence to hang his own shingle. Paula and Billy were cautiously optimistic for their son.

Trey broke the news to his parents regarding the football team celebration party at Julie James' house. "Everyone will be there. I'll be home on time." His curfew was midnight.

Billy had his doubts. "I don't know, Trey. You've been doing pretty good here lately. Going to a wild party probably isn't a good idea for you."

"It's not going to be a wild party. Just a bunch of us hanging out."

Paula shared Billy's concerns. "Trey, why would you even want to take the chance? You should know that sometimes you can be guilty by association. Why don't you have a few friends over and play video games?"

"My friends are going to the party. Why are you making this into such a big deal?"

With raised eyebrows, Paula deferred to Billy. "What do you think?"

One step at a time. Billy figured he needed to at least try to show some trust in his son. "Be home by midnight. If you see any trouble, walk away. No drinking and driving. The last thing your mom and I want is a call from the cops. Understood?"

"No problem. Stop worrying. See you guys later."

Trey's history was difficult to ignore. He hadn't made it easy for his parents to trust him, and each time he screwed up, it made it even more difficult. Trey was home by 11:30.

25

The fans were pressed tightly together on the aluminum benches of Trojan Stadium. It was standing room only on this bitterly cold Friday night of the Trojans' home playoff game. New Kent and Charles City were engaged in a defensive struggle, and the game was scoreless through the third quarter. With a little under two minutes to go in the game, the Trojans recovered a fumble on their own twenty-yard line. They promptly returned the favor by fumbling the ball right back to Charles City, who kicked the game-winning field goal on the last play of the game.

A dejected group of Trojan fans headed for their cars, and the heartbroken players and coaches assembled in the locker room. Coach Glass congratulated his squad. "I've never been any prouder of a team than I am right now. You boys just fought a heck of a fight, and we came up just a little bit short. There is absolutely no reason to hang your heads. I know you don't want to hear it right now, but in a few weeks, you'll be able to look back over this season and appreciate all that we accomplished."

The words rang hollow with the boys. Some couldn't fight back the tears of disappointment. Trey Pike rested the back of his head against the metal locker and squeezed his eyes tightly. He had a headache that wasn't subsiding. It had been bothering him since the midway point of the fourth quarter, but he didn't want to leave the game. A sudden wave of dizziness caused him to feel nauseated. He wobbled to the toilet and violently vomited. After another heave, he collapsed to the concrete floor. One of the assistant coaches raced to the field to alert the ambulance team, who rushed Trey to Williamsburg Regional Medical Center.

Several tests later, the emergency room doctor apprised Billy and Paula Pike of the situation. "Your son has suffered a concussion, and he's pretty dehydrated. We're giving him an IV to replenish his fluids. I think it's best to keep him under observation overnight, and if there are no complications, he'll be able to go home tomorrow."

But there were complications. Trey's headache was worse the following day, and there were intermittent waves of nausea. Billy tried to lighten the atmosphere by talking about the game, but Trey's response was chilling. "Dad, I don't even remember the game. The last thing I can remember is Coach Glass giving us a pep talk in the locker room before the game started."

Billy did his best to downplay the situation. "Don't worry about that right now. It'll come back to you."

"Do me a favor and close that blind. I can't take the sun. Too bright. Much better closed."

Trey's blood pressure was elevated, but his other vitals were in the normal ranges. If the nausea didn't subside and the vision remained abnormal, the doctor wanted to run more tests.

The sedative helped Trey get some much-needed sleep, but it was a restless night. By the next morning, the blurred vision had improved, and the nausea had stayed away.

The doctor peered down at Trey's chart. "Trey can go home this afternoon, but bring him back in if he experiences the nausea again. He should start feeling better day by day. It could take a couple of weeks before he returns to normal. This was a pretty nasty concussion. Just keep an eye on him. Absolutely no driving or strenuous activities for the next few days."

Billy and Paula agreed it would be best to keep Trey home for the remainder of the week. Paula would pick up his class assignments so he wouldn't fall too far behind. By Monday, Trey was still complaining about headaches. They weren't as intense as they had been early on, but they were persistent. By Wednesday, the headaches were less frequent. Trey's appetite was good, and everything seemed to be returning to normal.

Billy grilled Paula about Trey's condition. "Why didn't Trey go back to school today?"

"Billy, you have a short memory. We both agreed it was best to keep him home this week."

"I know what I agreed to, but he seems ok to me. I just saw him in the den playing video games. Are you telling me he can play video games but not sit at a desk at school?"

"The doctor said it was a serious concussion. He recommended that Trey take it easy for a while. Are you a doctor?"

"No, but I know you are a mother hen and perfectly comfortable to let Trey laze around the house all day long doing nothing."

"I'm not a mother hen, but I am a mother. It's just never good enough for you, Billy Pike. You're never happy unless you're bitching about something, and it's usually Trey."

"I had a couple of concussions back in high school. I was never out of commission this long."

"Good for you, Billy. I'm sure you're going to tell me you were tougher than Trey. It doesn't surprise me that you doubt his injury."

"I didn't say that. I'm just saying he knows how to take advantage of a situation, and he definitely knows which of your buttons to push."

"Yeah, Billy, and he's the only one that does."

Paula added peppermint to the vaporizer on Trey's dresser. A friend assured her that this home remedy cleared the sinuses, which would help prevent recurring headaches. Trey had a home remedy of his own that he was ready to try. He reached between the mattress and box springs and grabbed the zip lock bag. As he sat on the porch swing of the backyard deck, Trey inhaled deeply. After a couple more hits, the cannabis was taking effect. The headache was easing off as he relaxed into a slumber.

Trey went back to school the following Monday. Paula was so grateful that her friend's miracle remedy had cured her son's headaches.

26

After the second ring, Billy Pike checked the caller ID on his cell phone. Billy shook his head. It was Hank Foster, who was concerned that Billy had missed the last several meetings of the Patriots and wanted an explanation.

"Nothing to worry about, Hank. I just haven't had any time. There aren't enough hours in the day to get all my work done, and by the time I get home, I'm dead tired."

Hank Foster backed off, but Billy knew he would hear from him again. After the Washington, D.C., fiasco, Billy had lost interest in the Patriots and their agenda. He didn't plan on attending any more meetings, but he knew this was problematic. Hank Foster and several fellow Patriots were faithful customers of Billy. Terminating his membership would make Paula happy, but losing Hank's business would hurt. Billy didn't want Hank Foster as an enemy.

Grass-cutting season had slowed down as the winter months were approaching. In two more weeks, Billy could put the mowers in storage and prepare for his Christmas tree business. It was only six weeks of work, but the money was good, and most of his customers paid in cash. Sorry about that, Uncle Sam. The Spottswood family owned a strip mall shopping center near the outlet stores in Williamsburg, and for the past two years, they rented out a section of the parking lot for Billy Pike to sell his Christmas trees.

Billy drove over to the strip mall to mark the lot for the first delivery of trees. It would be a busy first few days as so many people had embraced the tradition of putting up their tree immediately following Thanksgiving. It was easy to get into the holiday spirit if you lived anywhere near Williamsburg because the city went all out for its grand illumination. Massive crowds drove in from distant locations. They all wanted to experience the festive air in the old historic city.

Billy wanted to finish marking the lot, but he had one more job to tend to. The Redskins were playing the Eagles, and he wanted to be sitting comfortably in his recliner when the game started. If he pushed himself, he'd finish the job with a little time to spare. To Billy Pike, it seemed that he was on the outside looking in. Everything was in slow motion. The embankment was steep, but it would only take a couple of run-throughs to cut the hill. He wouldn't have to waste valuable time using the push mower and weed whacker. The Redskins were waiting for their number one fan. The riding mower couldn't safely maneuver through the turn. Billy's right hand held the steering wheel as he extended his left arm to cushion the fall. He didn't have time to jump. He was in an awkward position as gravity was pulling the mower ever left. Billy rolled out of the seat and was flat on his back on the ground. The weight of the mower crashed down on Billy, instantly shattering his right shoulder. The pain was excruciating as he struggled to free himself from the machine. Seven minutes seemed like seven hours. A UPS driver spotted the accident and dialed 911. Billy Pike wouldn't be cheering on the burgundy and gold this evening, and he wouldn't be unloading Christmas trees any time soon. He was lucky to be alive.

27

Billy Pike's hospital stay was a painful five days. Any time he tried to move, the pain in his right shoulder was excruciating, and the meds being administered weren't doing the trick. To compound the situation, he had suffered two broken ribs and a lacerated kidney. The surgery to stop the internal bleeding had not been routine.

Five hundred blue spruce and Douglas fir trees were to be delivered to Billy's lot next week. Trey Pike had intended to help his dad here and there, but the scenario had suddenly changed dramatically.

Paula and Trey sat next to the hospital bed.

Billy was beside himself. "Can you believe this shit? I knew I shouldn't have tried that mower on that hill. But I was in a hurry to finish. I am such a dumbass. And now I'll be stuck with a ton of Christmas trees."

Paula jumped up and hurried to shut the door. "Billy! Keep your voice down."

"Keep my voice down? Do you have any idea the predicament I'm in?"

Trey quietly offered, "Dad, I can help out."

"Help out? Hey, Trey, I appreciate that, but I got to have

someone that is going to be there from noon to nine o'clock every day for the next six weeks."

"Yeah, I know. I can do it."

"Come on, Trey. You've never done anything like this in your life. It's out of the question."

"It's not rocket science, Dad. People are buying Christmas trees. Tie the tree on the car, and off they go."

"There's a lot more to it than that."

"Dad, you don't have any other options. I know I can do this."

Paula supported the plan. "Billy, you know that Trey is right. Unless you want to own a whole bunch of Christmas trees, this is your solution. For once in your life, trust your son."

Trey continued. "You know, Dad, Mr. Drummond isn't starting on a new house until late February. He might want to pick up a few extra bucks."

Some of Paula's words had stung Billy, but he knew that Trey was his only option.

The trees were cash on delivery. Paula went to the bank and got a cashier's check for five thousand dollars, which just about drained the joint savings account. By noon, Trey Pike was the proud supervisor of Happy Holidays Christmas Trees. Larry Drummond worked the daytime shift from noon to 4:00, and Trey relieved him when school adjourned. Both worked Saturdays and Sundays, which were, by far, the busiest days of the week. Trey had been right about one thing. It wasn't rocket science, and most of the time was spent waiting around for a customer to drop in.

Following two more deliveries of trees, Trey Pike's supervisory duties concluded on Christmas Eve. There were only about twenty trees that hadn't been sold, and Spottswood, Jr., had agreed to purchase them at cost so he could dump them in various spots in his property's lake. Supposedly, it was good for the vegetation and fish spawning.

Billy and Paula took care of the accounting. The six-week business had brought in nearly $52,000. After paying for the trees, lot rental to the Spottswoods, and labor costs, the net profit was almost $27,000. This good news helped soothe the ongoing pain in Billy Pike's shoulder. He owed a lot to Trey for stepping up in a crisis. Billy gave his son five thousand dollars and a brand-new Remington rifle for a job well done. A near tragedy had turned into a very merry Christmas for the Pike family. Was a happy New Year too much to ask for?

28

Randy Kean took a personal interest in his patients. He didn't take no for an answer, and he was consistent in pushing them out of their comfort zones. Randy would talk about the importance of maintaining a positive mental attitude, and he was big on goal setting. All successful people had goals, and working toward achieving the goal built strength of mind, body, and spirit. Billy Pike viewed Randy Kean as a necessary evil that had been put on the earth to torture innocent victims. Billy was seeing him for one of his regular physical therapy sessions.

"Dammit, that hurts. You must have been a drill sergeant in the Marines."

Randy laughed it off. "You know what they say. If there ain't no pain, then there ain't no gain. You're building back your strength and mobility."

"Yeah, right. You just get off killing your patients."

"Just keep your eye on the big goal, Billy."

"My big goal is that clock getting to eleven o'clock so I can get the hell out of here."

"There you go, Billy. Keep up that positive mental attitude. Great work today. You're getting stronger. That's for sure. Ok, see you in a couple of days."

"I can't wait."

Paula had served as a faithful nurse to her husband since the day he came home from the hospital, and fortunately, she was endowed with a great deal of patience. After the first week, Billy was like a caged lion. He was used to being out and about and managing his business. Spring was rapidly approaching, and Billy wasn't sure he would be physically able to do the work. He wasn't totally disabled, so he wouldn't be receiving any benefits from the government. He didn't own personal disability insurance, and he had never purchased worker's comp. There was money he had stashed away in the safe, but he had always counted that as retirement money. He had loyal customers, but he certainly couldn't expect them to forego their needs until he recovered. Trey could do the work, but Billy wanted him to graduate with his class, and he knew that Paula wouldn't consider taking Trey out of school. Realistically, Billy knew he had two options. One was to pay someone to do the work until he could return. The other was to find another job. Paula was pushing Billy toward the latter.

"Billy, you have to be realistic and sensible about this situation. Every year, the work is getting harder because you aren't getting any younger. Your physical therapy is going well, but there's no definite timetable for your full recovery. Maybe this was a wake-up call for you to do something else."

If he was going to be honest with himself, Billy knew Paula was right. Maybe he would talk to the Spottswoods and see if they could give him some direction.

It was late afternoon when the doorbell rang. Paula offered a blank expression to the two men who were flashing their badges.

"Mrs. Pike, I'm Special Agent Kane, and this is my partner, Special Agent Harding. If you have a few minutes, we need to ask you a few questions."

Billy Pike offered the same blank look as Paula invited the special agents to have a seat on the couch next to Billy's recliner.

"We need to ask some questions about your son, Trey. Is he home?"

Billy cut in. "What kind of questions do you need to ask Trey? Is he in some kind of trouble?"

"We're trying to find that out. We need to talk to Trey. When do you expect him home?"

Paula speed-dialed her son. He was on the way home now. Trey felt impending doom as he entered the family room.

"Trey, I'm Special Agent Kane, and this is Special Agent Harding. Our office is in Hampton Roads. We were contacted by the Williamsburg Police Department a few weeks ago. We work for the Drug Enforcement Administration."

Paula's and Billy's eyes were on Trey. Trey felt sick to his stomach.

Agent Kane continued. "Now, Mr. Pike, you own a Christmas tree lot over near the Target strip mall. Right?"

"I don't own it. I just rent the space around Christmas time."

"Well, you do run a business there. Right?"

"That's right. So?"

"So, we have reason to believe that some illegal drug activities occurred there while your business was operational."

"I don't know anything about any drug business. I don't think I can help you with any of this."

"You are telling me that you have no knowledge about the sale of any drugs from this property."

"I haven't even been able to work for the past month due to an accident."

"Sorry to hear that. Well, if you weren't there, who was?"

All eyes focused on Trey. Paula felt the need to protect her son. "Trey was working there to help his father, but Trey's not a drug dealer."

Agent Harding looked at Trey. "What can you tell us about this, Trey?"

"I don't know anything about any drug dealing."

His lack of eye contact with the agent made Billy feel uncomfortable.

The questioning turned to finances. Paula took the lead. "My husband and I handled all the orders, payments, and deposits. I can assure you that everything is legitimate."

"Maybe so, Mrs. Pike. That's something we will definitely need to look at."

Billy felt that the agent's tone was condescending. "What do you mean by saying maybe so? Are you saying my wife's a liar?"

"I'm not calling anybody anything, Mr. Pike. Just doing our job. We'll be back in touch. Here's my card. Be sure to contact us if there's anything you think we should know. Oh, and just an FYI. You should know that methamphetamine is considered a controlled drug in the State of Virginia. Possession and distribution are prosecuted to the letter of the law. Penalties range from five to fifty years in prison. We appreciate your hospitality. Have a nice day."

29

The interrogation from the DEA agents was bad enough, but the grilling Trey received from Billy and Paula Pike was worse.

"You see, Paula. I knew things were going too good to be true. I knew some kind of shit was ready to hit the fan. And here we are. The shit has definitely hit the fan. This is a small community we live in, and now our names are going to get dragged through the mud."

Paula said, "You're worried about our reputation? How about prison? Prison!" She looked at her son. "Trey, if you know anything at all about this, now is the time to come clean."

"What do you want me to say? I don't know anything about this."

Billy wasn't convinced. "How about that damn Larry Drummond? You know the agents are going to talk to him. He's got the biggest mouth on the planet. Does he know anything about this?"

"How am I supposed to know what Mr. Drummond knows? All I can tell you is that I haven't done anything wrong."

Two days later, Paula received a phone call from Special

Agent Kane, who conveyed that he would need to take a look at the financial transactions of the tree sales. He could get a warrant for further investigation, or she could cooperate. Paula considered asking if she should seek legal counsel, but she didn't have anything to hide and didn't want to raise more suspicion. She would have the information ready by the next day.

The receipts for inventory showed there had been three deliveries of trees. Paula explained the wholesale and retail numbers. She pointed out that most of the sales were made in cash. There wasn't any hanky panky going on as far as the spreadsheet showed, but Agent Kane wanted to discuss the bank account. Billy had opened a separate checking account when he started the business two years ago. Paula entered her password to the online banking account and browsed through the history of deposits and withdrawals. Nothing seemed to be out of order.

Billy said, "Show him the other accounts. We got nothing to hide."

Agent Kane said, "That won't be necessary, but does Trey have an account?"

Paula nodded. "It's a joint checking account with me. Let me log in." Paula felt a numbness engulf her body as her throat tightened. Her eyes couldn't hide her surprise. She struggled to speak the words, "The balance is at zero!"

It had all been withdrawn that afternoon. Paula and Billy stared at each other, but they had no explanation for Agent Kane.

"Trey should be home soon. I'm sure there's a reasonable explanation to all of this."

Agent Kane couldn't wait to hear the details.

Paula and Billy speed-dialed Trey, but each time, it went straight to voice mail. He was probably over at a friend's house playing the latest version of *Grand Theft Auto*. Billy got in touch with Larry Drummond.

"Hey, Larry. Billy Pike here. I'm trying to track down Trey. Is he working with you today?"

"Hey, Billy. No, he's not with me. I haven't seen him since we closed down the tree sales."

"Ok, Larry. If you see him, tell him to call me."

"Sure will. Is everything ok with Trey?"

"Yeah. Everything's fine. Thanks. Talk to you soon."

Paula was getting more nervous by the minute. "Maybe his phone is out of juice."

After thirty minutes of trying to contact Trey, Agent Kane was out of patience and tired of making small talk. "Just call me when you find Trey. He's going to need to answer some questions."

The Pikes promised that they would.

By 10:00 that evening, Paula was in full panic mode, and Billy wasn't far behind. Paula texted the situation to her daughter, but Hannah hadn't talked to Trey since spring break. Billy stepped out onto the screened-in porch and decided to call Larry Drummond again.

"Hey, Larry. Sorry to bug you again."

"No problem, Billy. Have you talked to Trey?"

"Not yet. That's the reason I'm calling you back. I need to ask you a couple of questions. Did you notice any funny business going on at the tree lot over the past few weeks?"

"I can guarantee you I wasn't involved in anything out of line."

"I'm not saying you were, Larry. I'm not suspecting you of anything. I'm asking if you saw Trey involved in anything suspicious."

"Billy, I don't want to get Trey in any trouble."

"I know that, Larry, but did you see anything I should know about?"

There was an uncomfortable silence until Larry replied.

"Well, do you remember that dude Trey used to hang out with? Dylan Day?"

Billy and Paula remembered him well. The very mention of his name sent chills down their spines.

Dylan Day was that guy that parents wanted their children to avoid at all costs. Dylan had been dealt a pretty lousy hand in life. He never knew his father, and his mother had died as a result of a heroin overdose when Dylan was three. Neither of his aunts had wanted custody, so he had gotten traded around to several foster homes. After his third breaking-and-entering conviction at age thirteen, the judge sent him to the James City Juvenile Detention Center. Two years later, he had been released and definitely not rehabilitated. Between the sexual abuse and the frequent drug use at the center, Dylan had been in worse shape than when he had entered the facility.

Another foster family took him in, and Dylan had started school again. His behavior in school was usually disruptive, and most of his curriculum was in special education. Sophomore year, he and Trey Pike had shared the same English class. Both boys were loners for the most part and didn't really fit in with any of the popular cliques.

Trey had bought his first bag of pot from Dylan Day. The social users and the hardcore stoners bought their grass from Dylan. He had a successful operation going and was happy to cut Trey in on the action. Trey wasn't the entrepreneur that Dylan was, but he established a steady clientele that put a few bucks in his pocket.

Dylan had dropped out of school during the second semester of sophomore year and graduated to more profitable consumer goods. Methamphetamine was the drug of choice in many of the rural communities, and Dylan manned a territory for a local distributor. He had wanted to cut Trey in on the profits, but Trey had been reluctant. Trey's thinking was that no one would get too bent out of shape if you got caught with weed, but meth was a totally different animal. Dylan didn't pressure Trey but told him to hit him up if he ever changed his mind and wanted to make some real "gangster money."

Billy let out an extended sigh. "Yeah, Larry. I remember Dylan Day. Who could ever forget Dylan Day?"

"Well, Dylan hung around the lot a few times, mainly evening time. I probably saw him three or four times. I didn't see him causing any trouble."

"How about Trey? Was Trey hanging with Dylan?"

"I ain't gonna say he never spoke to him, but it wasn't like they were attached at the hip. You know, Billy, Trey ain't nothing like that Day boy. Trey's a good kid, and I can tell you he did a damn good job with those trees. You should be proud of him."

"Yeah, Larry. I appreciate that. Is there anything else you can think of?"

"No. That's about it. I'll let you know if I can think of anything else."

"Ok, Larry. Thanks."

Billy Pike hung his head and began to cry. He desperately needed to talk to his son.

30

Trey Pike examined the tattoo on his left shoulder as he studied his profile in the mirror. It was a Tyrannosaurus Rex inked in green and black. "RIP" and "In Memoriam" were arced in jet-black block letters across Trey's upper back. Paula had always raised objections to any tattoo.

"Trey, this is a permanent choice. What if you're sorry down the road? Why don't you wait?"

But Trey hadn't waited. He had a difficult time focusing on the next day, much less years into the future. If he survived the next few days, maybe he would return to the parlor for some more dark images. In a way that he couldn't explain, the pain of the needle brought him some degree of pleasure. It was a feeling he would never share with anyone else. Trey had packed lightly. A couple of changes of clothes, some personal hygiene items, a family picture from his childhood days, and his firepower. A thirty-eight-caliber handgun and his Remington rifle. He had gone to the bank earlier in the day to withdraw his money. Hundreds and fifties totaling more than ten thousand dollars. The warning words of the DEA agent steadily replayed in his mind: "Possession and distribution of meth are prosecuted to the letter of the law. Penalties range from five to fifty years in prison."

The agents had probably been building a case for a long time. They had probably already talked to Larry Drummond, who had most likely connected Trey to Dylan Day. Certainly, they knew about the ten thousand dollars, and Trey had no believable story to account for it. He could turn himself in and tell the truth, but he knew that Dylan was associated with some dangerous people. Trey thought about contacting Dylan Day, but it was too risky. He considered putting the barrel of the thirty-eight in his mouth, but the image of his mother's mourning made him pause. She would forgive him and still love him, but he knew he had burned the last bridge with his father. Five to fifty years in prison. But Trey wasn't the supplier or the distributor. Hell, it wasn't even his lot from where the meth had been sold. But Trey had known what had been going on. Dylan Day had approached Trey with a business proposition. They weren't close friends. Hadn't even seen one another in two years. Trey knew he should have told Dylan thanks but no thanks, but he had been careless.

Dylan's confident promises now made Trey wince. "Believe me, Trey. No one will ever know. Who's gonna be eyeballing a Christmas tree lot? There's nothing you have to do. Just let me do my thing and look the other way. Santa Claus will fill your stocking with a lot of goodies when it's over."

Dylan was right about the goodies. Trey hadn't thought twice when he accepted the money, but he knew he had made a huge mistake by depositing the money into the joint checking account.

Trey stared at his cell phone as it stopped ringing and went to voicemail. He had lost count of the unanswered attempts from Mom, Dad, Hannah, Larry Drummond, and one number he didn't recognize. Probably Agent Kane or Harding. He summoned the nerve to call his mom.

"Hey, Mom. Just want to let you and Dad know that I'm alright, and I know I really screwed up. I love you guys." He didn't wait for a response.

Paula repeated her son's name over and over, but Trey was gone. Her worst thoughts paralyzed her. Would she ever see her son again?

Special Agents Kane and Harding sat in the Pikes' den and wanted any information Billy and Paula could offer.

Billy's tone and demeanor were even less cordial than the previous meeting. "Business must be mighty slow. You guys think Trey is a major criminal or what? We told you we'd contact you if we found out anything about his whereabouts. I know my son is no altar boy, but he's certainly not a dangerous criminal."

"Mr. Pike, no one is saying that, but we have a job to do. We know that there was illegal drug activity being conducted on that tree lot. Your son was managing that tree lot. We know that Trey knows Dylan Day. It's imperative that we talk to Trey. Get it?"

"Yeah, we get it. We've told you all we know. Have you talked to Dylan Day? He's the guy you should be focusing in on."

"Mr. Pike, I think we know how to do our job, but thanks for your advice."

Paula interrupted. "That was Trey that just called."

The agents were all ears. "And?"

"And nothing. All he said is that he's alright. Then he hung up. That's it. Nothing else."

Billy Pike slouched in his chair and prayed for a miracle.

31

The City of Richmond Salvage Center had a steady flow of customers. It was a car enthusiast's dream come true. Parts from most makes of cars and trucks could be found at the Salvage Center. Trey Pike needed to ditch his truck, but he needed transportation. Nervously, he approached a man who was taking tires off a late-model Mustang.

"Do you work here?"

"That's what they tell me. What do you want?"

"I saw a few cars in the front parking lot area. Are any of them for sale?"

"You gotta talk to Sly about that. He's probably in the office over there."

"Sly?"

"Yeah. Just ask for Sly."

Trey made his way to the office. He thought to himself, "If Mom thinks my bedroom is a mess, she should take a look at this place. What a pigsty." Trey tapped on the door. There sat a slovenly-looking man wearing a dirty tank top and smoking a cheap cigar. The metal desk was covered with disorderly piles of papers, order forms and invoices. The stench from cigar smoke was thick in the room. Trey's first instinct was to walk away, but the burly man looked his way.

"You need something?"

"Are you Sly?"

"Maybe. Who's asking?"

"Joe. Joe Johnson."

"Ok, Joe. What's up?"

"I was looking at the Toyota out front. Is it for sale?"

"Everything's for sale, Joe Johnson. That Camry runs good. Just picked it up last week."

"How much?"

"Well, I got three thousand in it. I got to make a little money, so I'd let it go for thirty-five."

"How about a trade?"

Sly frowned and asked, "Trade? What kind of trade?"

"I got that black pickup out there."

"Give me your keys, and let my guy drive it." Sly yelled out, "Hey, Shorty. Come here a minute."

Shorty was the guy that had directed Trey to Sly.

Sly tossed the keys to Shorty. "Take that black truck out for a few miles, and let me know what you think."

Upon his return, Shorty reported, "Runs good. Little bit of shake in the right front. Probably needs alignment. No big thing."

Sly looked suspiciously at Trey. "So, Joe, what's the deal? How come you want to trade something that's worth more than what you're going to get in return?"

"I just need something different."

"You just need something different. I think you're full of shit."

Trey turned to walk away, but Sly stopped him.

"Hold on a minute, Joe. As if that's really your damn name. I'm supposing you're in some kind of trouble. Some kind of situation. You got the title with you?"

Trey shook his head. "Let's just forget it. Sorry I wasted your time."

Sly never could count the number of shady deals he had made over the years. What was the harm in one more? "Ok, Mr. Joe Johnson. Here's the keys to the Camry. And remember, I ain't never seen you before in my whole life." Sly threw in a set of Connecticut license plates on the house.

Trey made a stop at Grover's Army Surplus and purchased ammunition for both guns. He ran into a local grocery store and purchased some nutrition.

Trey checked into the Royal Motel on Jefferson Davis Highway in Richmond. It was a real shithole that patronized drug addicts and prostitutes. He was confident that he could hide out there for a few days. The cops would avoid this place if possible. Trey stared at the shattered television screen. There was no use in reporting it to the manager. Hell, it had been hard enough to get a couple of clean bath towels. Trey had paid cash for a three-night stay so he didn't have to worry about anyone tracking a credit card transaction.

Trey recounted some of the mistakes he had made in his lifetime. He wished there was no one in his life who loved him. His mother was the only one who said she understood him, but she really had no clue at all. His sister was unconditional in her love for her brother, but it was often too painful to be around her. Trey could never measure up to Hannah. He sensed that he was routinely held up in comparison to her. Surely, everyone could see how perfect Hannah was and what a screw-up Trey was. And then there was his father.

If Trey could have ever pleased him, maybe things would have turned out better, but Trey knew he was a big disappointment to Billy. He had tried with good intentions to rise to the occasion to help his dad when he needed him most, and he had actually succeeded in doing an admirable job of managing the Christmas tree lot. Admirable, with the exception of quality control. He knew he should have told Dylan Day to take a hike. He remembered the words of his parents. Ever since he could remember, they had told him to be smart when choosing your friends. "Lots of times, you can be guilty by association."

It had been the same in high school. Trey had known that Dylan Day was trouble from the get-go. But Dylan gave attention to Trey. Attention that he had rarely received throughout his life. Trey played football, but he didn't hang out with the jocks. Trey slid by with average to below-average grades, so he wasn't popular with the teachers. Trey didn't even get the time of day from the nerds. He was an outsider and didn't know how to fit in. Trey knew right from wrong, but he ignored it time and time again. Trey knew it was his fault that he had allowed Dylan Day to set up shop at the Christmas tree lot. Trey wasn't going to make any excuses, and he wasn't seeking forgiveness from anyone. There was an inner rage that he didn't want to suppress any longer. He didn't want anyone to care about him. Trey had convinced himself that it was best to be alone. He would move to another part of the country. Maybe even Mexico. How hard would it be to just disappear and start a new life? He certainly would never appear on the FBI's Ten Most Wanted list.

Trey stretched out on the rickety double bed and closed his eyes. He only needed one round of his ammunition to end his inner conflict, but he couldn't get his mother out of his mind. After tossing and turning for an hour, he sat on the edge of the bed and composed a letter to his parents and his sister. Trey folded the letter, placed it in his backpack, and began to cry.

32

Billy Pike's concerns about Larry Drummond's propensity to run his mouth had come true. Good old Larry had managed to let the cat out of the bag around several members of the Patriots for Freedom. It didn't take long before the Pikes were receiving a barrage of phone calls. Some people expressing their heartfelt concern and support, and others hoping for some juicy details. At least it wasn't a surprise when Hank Foster rang the doorbell.

She had to grit her teeth, but Paula invited Hank in. It was hard to be cordial. "Hi, Hank. Do you want to talk to Billy?"

"If it wouldn't be intruding, Paula, I'd like to."

You can't imagine how much of an intrusion you are, you racist asshole. Paula restrained her true feelings. "Right this way. Billy's in the den."

"Hey, Billy. Just wanted to come by and tell you and Paula how sorry I am to hear about Trey. A bunch of the other boys in the Patriots are real concerned, too. We all know this has got to be a rough time for your family."

Maybe Hank Foster's words were filled with sincerity, but Billy didn't receive them in that manner. Billy only nodded.

Hank continued. "Just want to let you know that we're all

here for you, and I can guarantee you that nobody blames you and Paula for all this mess."

That would be the sentence from Hank Foster that lit the fire in Billy Pike.

"Well, you know, Hank, I can't begin to tell you how much it warms my heart that you and the other Patriots don't think any less of me. As a matter of fact, I was just telling Paula that I hoped our good name was still held in high regard by one of the most ignorant, racist groups of people that I have ever known. Hopefully, Hank, you're smart enough to understand sarcasm when you hear it."

Hank Foster's face was beet red as Billy continued. "Ever since that rally I took my son to in Washington, I've been thinking a lot about my life, and one of my regrets was ever getting involved with your group. You guys got it all wrong. It took me some time to realize it, but better late than never. I jeopardized the safety of my own flesh and blood to go to a rally with a bunch of radicals."

Hank exploded. "What radicals? We're the ones trying to fight the radicals. All of them that are trying to ruin our country and way of life."

"Oh, what a crock of shit. You're not worried about the well-being of your country. For whatever reason, you hate Black people, and you mask it by talking about a bunch of other issues. Just be honest. This is all about Black and White."

Paula was smiling as she waited for more.

Billy continued, "You come over here acting so concerned about my family, especially Trey. What the hell are you concerned about? Were you so concerned when I nearly killed myself a few weeks ago? I don't remember you or any of the Patriots banging on my door to see if we needed anything. Oh, by the way, the UPS guy that called 911? He was an African American. You know, one of those people that's dragging our country down. Thank God for Paula and Trey. I don't know what I would have done without them. It took me some time, but I've finally realized that my family is the most important thing to me in this world. I want to be a better husband to Paula and a better father to Hannah and Trey. I don't have any more interest in hanging out with the Williamsburg Klan."

Paula was moved to tears and had never been prouder of her husband.

Billy said, "Now, Hank, you can show yourself out and be sure not to worry yourself about me or my family anymore."

It was a rarity for Hank Foster to be stricken speechless. He gathered some composure. "Billy, I think once you've cooled down, you'll see how wrong you've been today. And I really don't appreciate the way you've talked to me, and I can assure you the Patriots will welcome you back when you've come to your senses."

Billy Pike rose from his recliner, stepped toward Hank Foster, and stared daggers. "I don't need any time to do any more thinking. I will never be associated with you again. Take a hike."

Paula and Billy held hands as they watched Hank Foster waddle to his truck. She embraced her husband and looked into his bloodshot eyes. Eyes that welcomed her back into his arms. Eyes that longed to hear some news about their son. This was the man that Paula had fallen in love with. This was the man that Paula had married. This was the man Paula had feared she had lost. They cried together and prayed that Trey would find his way home.

33

He sat on the plastic bucket and surveyed the parking lot. Only a handful of cars, but it was still early. The Pop-Tarts and Red Bull had done the trick. His stomach wasn't growling, and the caffeine was a welcome jolt. There weren't going to be any interruptions this time, and he wasn't going to surrender to any hesitations, second-guessing, or feelings of guilt. If any heating and air conditioning repairmen showed up, they would be part of the collateral damage. He was in charge today, and people were going to stand up and notice his power. They were going to be held accountable for the pain he had had to endure. There would only be one vitals check this day, and that was only due to habit. One-fifteen over seventy-four and forty-eight. Blood pressure and heart rate were good to go. He disassembled the rifle and put it back together. Scope was functional, and ammo was in place. Plenty of ammo. Locked, loaded, and ready to go. He'd had concerns with the timing of the escape route in the original plans, but that was no longer a point of concern. There would be no escape today. It had been too mentally exhausting to contemplate future missions. Better to have one grand display. Law enforcement officers, first responders, news reporters, Leann

Walker, and her whole damn family. All were welcome to take part in today's activities. Have a tailgate party and enjoy the fireworks. Guaranteed to get your money's worth. Fifteen minutes until showtime. The parking lot was starting to fill. He set his sights exactly on the front doors of Damon's Fine Wardrobes. A dozen customers had made a line, waiting for 9:00 A.M. There wouldn't be a limit of five targets today. He would pull the trigger until he didn't want to pull the trigger anymore. So many targets and so much time. At least twenty-five people were now waiting in the line. Maybe the husbands would be happy that the credit cards wouldn't be used today.

The first shot shattered the upper spine of the second lady in line. Pandemonium set in when the fifth victim collapsed on the concrete walkway. He paused as he smiled at the screaming that filled the air. Twelve down as he stood to stretch. After taking a sip of Red Bull, he was back on attack. The twenty-first casualty was a young mother who was frantically pushing her two children back into the minivan. He shot out the rear window of a Jeep that was trying to exit the lot.

As he sat on the bucket, he pulled out his smartphone. It hadn't taken long for his mission to become breaking news. He looked forward to seeing the local news teams arrive. He would love to have them as guests. All were welcome. Within an hour, local, state, and federal authorities were on the scene. It wouldn't be long before the helicopter appeared.

He smiled as he heard the officer on the bullhorn. Surrender wasn't going to be an option. There wouldn't be any negotiations. The rotors of the helicopter whipped round and round. He dropped his rifle and pulled out an American flag from his backpack. He stared into the gray sky and waved the flag from side to side. The officer's words from the bullhorn to drop his weapon made no impression on him. Dropping the flag, he quickly snatched the Remington and took dead aim at the helicopter. Before he could set his sight, a shot rang out from the rooftop of Damon's Fine Wardrobes. The sniper's bullet was true as he collapsed next to his bucket. The mass murderer's name would not be released until family members could be contacted.

34

Local, state, and national news teams flooded the shopping center parking lot. The authorities were giving their best efforts to crowd control. Hundreds of citizens wanted to get an up-front and personal feel for the killing field. People were snapping pictures with their cellphones and forwarding them to friends and posting them on every social media outlet. There were more than one hundred fifty law enforcement officers and at least another fifty first responders on the scene. The casualty count was at thirty. Twenty-one dead and nine wounded.

Captain Ronald Kincaid of the Williamsburg police force was the official spokesman for the crime scene. It was mostly "We can't comment on that until we get additional information" and "We are not able to release the name of the shooter at this time." There was no shortage of reporters throughout the lot. All knew this would be the leading story for the next forty-eight hours. The nightly news and talk show hosts could reschedule their guests for the foreseeable future. Leading mental health experts would be able to offer analysis on why another mass murder had taken place in the U.S. Once again, our citizens could have heated debates about gun control, background checks, and the Second Amendment. And then there would be the multiple opportunities for human interest stories. Each and every victim's loved ones would be bombarded with interview requests. There would certainly be a book written and possibly even a dramatic movie or miniseries within the next few months.

By noon, Captain Kincaid had a breaking news statement to reveal the killer's identity. He had been born and raised in a community near Williamsburg. The captain could not report a motive at this time, but the killer had left a letter that had been found in his backpack. He was sorry for the disappointment he had been to his family, and he was sorry for all the pain he had caused them through the years. He wanted his mother, father, and sister to know that he loved them. Captain Kincaid took a deep breath and prepared for the onslaught of questions as he revealed the name of the killer. The camera crews raced to their vans. They couldn't wait to get their microphones in the faces of the killer's family.

35

Hannah Pike had made the trip home from college to be with her parents. Being unaware of Trey's location for the past two days had been gut-wrenching. Billy wanted to hop in his truck and drive to who knows where. All three wanted to escape, but knew they needed to be strong for each other. The Pike family was passing time like many folks around the country. The shooting spree was being broadcast as the Mall Massacre. The eyes of the nation were on Williamsburg.

The silence in the Pikes' den was deafening until Hannah voiced what had crossed all their minds. "There's no way the killer is Trey. I know my brother, and despite all his problems, I know he would never hurt another soul."

Hannah pulled out a family photo album from the bookshelf. It consisted mostly of birthday and Christmas pictures. There was Billy in his T-Rex costume for Trey's birthday party. Another photo showed Hannah and Trey playing in the backyard tree fort. There was Paula kissing Billy under the mistletoe. Billy had videotaped some family get-togethers when the kids were younger. It had been years since they had sat together as a family to reminisce. The DVD brought some smiles and plenty of tears.

They all braced themselves when they heard the slam of the car door. Paula walked toward the front door but could hear the opening of the back door. All three sets of eyes darted back and forth to one another. Hannah jumped to her feet and embraced her brother. Trey Pike had spent the morning in a sports bar. All sixteen televisions were reporting on the mall massacre. Trey ordered a Coke and studied the screens. So much death. So much sadness. So many families that would be torn apart. Many would never be able to pick up the pieces to start again. He was overcome by a deep sense of guilt.

The news anchorman announced that Captain Kincaid was ready to make an announcement.

"I can report that the identity of the presumed assassin is Tyler Wood. We have contacted his family, and I ask that you respect their privacy during this ongoing investigation. I will take your questions at this time."

For the last forty-eight hours, Trey Pike had made his loved ones live through hell on earth. The mall massacre was a symbol of horror for so many, but in a strange way, it had served as an impetus for Trey Pike. Sitting in that sports bar, he had intently watched the unfolding tragedy. Trey had focused on the aftermath that this troubled young man had left as his legacy. Surely, Trey's troubles were not in the same category as Tyler Wood's, but the massacre had caused him to look at his life in a more meaningful light. As he looked at the smiles on the faces of his loved ones, he was certain that he had made the right choice. And then the unexpected happened. Billy Pike embraced his son and whispered words that Trey would remember for the rest of his life. "I love you, Trey."

Trey took the initiative to contact Special Agent Kane. The result was his arrest on the charge of distribution of a controlled substance. The judge agreed to grant bail and release

Trey until his trial date. Billy hired an attorney to represent Trey.

The case was heard by a judge, not a jury. At the sentencing phase of the trial, Billy, Paula, and Hannah held hands as the judge prepared to announce his ruling. Trey was visibly shaking as the judge stared at him.

"Trey Pike. It is the judgment of this court that you willingly aided and abetted in the crime of distribution of a controlled substance. The prosecution is seeking a penalty of incarceration for a period of five years, and to be perfectly frank, I do not view their request as unreasonable."

Trey's mouth was as dry as dust, and it was a struggle to remain standing.

The judge continued. "I was very impressed with some of the character witnesses that spoke on your behalf, and I conducted a thorough review of your background. Except for a couple of speeding tickets, you have a clean record. I also considered the fact that you eventually cooperated with the authorities. Therefore, this court rules that you are sentenced to three years with twenty-four months suspended in the James City Jail. You will begin serving your six months on July 1 of this year. And one final word of caution to you, Trey. The least little slip up on your part, and you will serve the entirety of your three-year sentence. Am I understood?"

Trey Pike's understanding was clearer than it had ever been.

36

Three Years Later

Larry Drummond eyed the crown molding and admired the beautiful hardwood floors. The open floor plan was spacious, and there were plenty of windows to capture the morning and afternoon sun. It was Trey Pike's first spec house. Billy had loaned him the money to purchase the lot and had co-signed the construction loan. Trey, Billy, and Larry stood on the back deck and enjoyed some Coors Lights. Larry praised the work.

"Damn, Trey. I got to tell you something. This is a hell of a lot better than my first house. Really super job."

Billy's injured shoulder was mostly operational, and his new employer was Pike's Custom Homes. Dad had made the decision to bet on his son this time. Billy was able to appreciate the fact that recent events had been turning points in both his and Trey's lives.

Billy made an unexpected toast. "Here's to Dylan Day."

Trey frowned, and Larry scratched his head in bewilderment.

"Yeah, you heard me right. They say something good can come from something bad. I was real lucky with that lawn mower accident. It was bad, but it could have been a whole lot worse. I got to be honest with you. I had serious doubts about you guys being able to manage the tree lot, especially Trey. And then when all the crap went down with cops at my house, Dylan Day and Trey disappearing. Well, let's just say I wasn't really happy with life in general. But life can be funny. The more I thought about everything that had happened, the angrier I got, and then I got to the point where I wasn't mad anymore. I was sad. I was sad that my wife was so afraid. I was sad that my little girl was so upset, and I was terrified that I'd never see my son again. I realized that all I wanted was my family again. Somewhere along the way, I had forgotten what was important in this life. We all just wanted Trey to come home."

Trey broke the seriousness of the moment. "Well then, here's to Dylan Day. I sure hope I don't ever see him again."

All three chuckled as they clinked their cans together. Billy and Trey Pike were on their personal roads to redemption. This was a good day to celebrate.

About Atmosphere Press

Founded in 2015, Atmosphere Press was built on the principles of Honesty, Transparency, Professionalism, Kindness, and Making Your Book Awesome. As an ethical and author-friendly hybrid press, we stay true to that founding mission today.

If you're a reader, enter our giveaway for a free book here:

SCAN TO ENTER
BOOK GIVEAWAY

If you're a writer, submit your manuscript for consideration here:

SCAN TO SUBMIT
MANUSCRIPT

And always feel free to visit Atmosphere Press and our authors online at atmospherepress.com. See you there soon!

About the Author

An independent investment advisor and former high school history teacher, **BLAND WEAVER** is an elder at the Gayton Kirk Presbyterian Church and president of the Kiwanis Club of Tuckahoe. Bland enjoys racquetball, swimming and taking long walks with his faithful chocolate lab, Lovey. Bland lives in Glen Allen, Virginia, with his wife, Joy, who is the inspiration for his writing. They have two sons, Eli and Zachary.